Sheep & The Wolves

Ifalade TaShia Asanti

Sheep & the Wolves
Published by Noble Trinity Publishing/Motherland Press
ISBN 978-0-9789869-5-7

Cover Design by GermanCreative
Author images provided by Ifalade Ta'Shia Asanti

Every book published by Noble Trinity Publishing and Motherland Press is printed and manufactured in the United States of America.

Also By Ifalade TaShia Asanti
The Sacred Five
The Sacred Door
The Bones Do Talk
The Master Breakthrough
Fluid: Out of Darkness Comes Light

Foreword

Across America and around the globe, drug trafficking drives a myriad of tragedies. From children being orphaned, homelessness of youth and families and higher instances of violent crimes. Sadly, the use of crack cocaine and Ecstasy also known as *E,* as well as street concoctions such a *Lean*, continue to steal and destroy lives.

In the hope of overcoming what is often generational poverty, people are drawn to selling drugs for the quick come up. While neighborhood dealers do become temporarily, "ghetto rich," most end up in jail or other institutions or worse, dead.

It is primarily the distributors of street drugs who are the major recipient of drug trafficking wealth. They amass millions while remaining virtually invisible under the protection of the powers that be.

Having had close friends and family members who've been impacted by America's drug epidemic, I have witnessed the destructive nature of addiction to drugs and its sister, alcohol. My prayer is that this book will be an inspiring healing agent for those who lives have been shattered. I impart a secondary message to addicts and alcoholics that it's never too late to seek help and that change is always possible.

Ifalade TaShia Asanti

If you or a loved one are struggling with issues related to drug addiction or alcoholism, the numbers below can assist you in finding help.

Cocaine Anonymous
https://ca.org/

Alcoholics Anonymous
https://www.aa.org/

National Drug Helpline
http://drughelpline.org/

Substances Abuse & Mental Health
https://www.samhsa.gov/find-help/national-helpline

Addiction Resources
https://addictionresource.com/addiction-and-rehab-hotlines/

DEDICATIONS

This book is dedicated to my daughter, D.A.Y. (Kombo) May you always remember what is truly important in life and that is the people we love and the joy we spread. Love fearlessly and live YOUR life like its golden. Your Mommy loves you like cornbread, macaroni and cheese, collard greens, peach cobbler and candied yams! Grandma kisses to all my grandchildren.

To my love, D. Pepper Massey who was a key visionary in the birth of the Sheep and The Wolves. I love you beyond life honey. Thank you for being the first ears and eyes for this and every book. Thank you for always believing in me and my dreams. You are a perfect beat over a tight lyric. ETL

And to my love, Jacquelyn "Pinky" Kennedy. Thank you for pushing me to put me (and my writing) first and teaching me the importance of unconditional love. Thank you for listening to me talk about these characters on those long road trips! I love you in spirit, heart and truth. Forever baby...Puma

To My Family:
Francis, Monique, Walker, Cheryl, Toni, Jason, Shawntel, Lori, Audrey, Lori, Egiyah, Devin, Lauren and all those connected to me by blood/ancestry. I love you forever always.

To my Spiritual Teachers & Supporters:
Oloye Ifa Karade, Betty Henderson, Iyanifa Ifalola, Awobemiga Bogunmbe, Awo Ifasola, Iya (Queen Mother) Oyafunmike Ogunlano. You are my air...

To My Friends For Life
Iya Nanina, Iyanifa Senakhu, Iyanifa Oshunike, Iyanifa Oshara, Iya Osunlade (Yetunde), Sis. Alexis, Iyanifa Onifa, Cassandra Reed, Cleo Manago, Laurence Pinckney, Jeffrey King

To My Babies and Godchildren
There are too many to list here. If I missed you, know you are among the names listed below. I love you for life. Zannie, Deborah, Denise, Carla, Crystal, Tyler, Roxanne, Lillie. And all my Ifa Godchildren but in particular-Lou, Julia, Geevani, Jenenne, Nicole S, Iyalosa, Rory, Candis, LaWanda, Almeta, Michael, Ifasina, Luna, Circe, Preston, Wanjira, Sangotoke, Amy, Kamil, Sara, Brandy, Autumn, Josue, Stone, Zayvier.

To My Fans & Writing Family-Without you, there would be no *Sheeps and The Wolves, Bones Do Talk, The Seer, The Sacred Door, Master Breakthrough, Fluid: Out of Darkness Comes Light, Tapestries of Faith or Letters To My Bu*

One

In another world, Bethsheba Dorothy Ransome would've been a goddess, a revered deity like the West African God Oshun. But in this life Sheba was a wolf, a no-nonsense alpha who led her pack without mercy.

Sheba's way of life was governed by three animalistic laws—

Destroy one's enemies.
Preserve your position as leader of the pack.
Protect the pack at all costs.

In that order.

Sheba had been trained by the gurus. Two of the most ruthless wolfs the streets of Los Angeles had produced.

The first to introduce her to the game was the womb that conceived and birthed her. Dorothy Oziah Ransome—the world had given her the sobriquet Mamadee. Mamadee was the daughter of two good Christian parents who were as Godly as the devil himself. Miss Dorothy was a master at the game of swindling. It would take at least two generations of do-gooders to clear the karma Lady D had accumulated with her heartless schemes.

Sheba's second teacher was John Henry Carter, a six-footer with a body like a wrestler. Sheba's beau was a man with no compassion or morals. A man who had turned his back on his family to maintain his kingdom—a kingdom that had long since been decimated by his rivals.

Despite his denounced status, Sheba worshipped the ground John Henry walked on. If he rang her phone she'd stop whatever she was doing to talk to him. If he dropped by for one of his rare visits, you'd think Martin Luther King was in the living room.

When John Henry came to visit Sheba even did something she hardly ever did—she cooked. Not some trite menu with store-bought ingredients. Sheba cooked by scratch using her mother's family recipes. Stuffed Cornish hens, candied yams, collard greens and hot water corn bread. On his last visit, she'd prepared her Granny's famous peach cobbler with the homemade crust. John Henry's thank you was a ghetto sentiment that'd made Raymond—Raymond was Sheba's current man--want to snatch his heart out of his chest.

Toothpick in hand, cleaning his pearly whites he uttered, "Damn, Sheba. That food was on point. But the view while you were cooking was even better. Nothing like watching a woman's ass move around the kitchen."

Sheba ignored his crass comments but Raymond put him in check with a quick.

Raymond stared the old wolf down and told him. "Told you before, don't be playing with my woman. If you can't show respect, don't come to my house."

"Man, what you getting all riled up for? Me and She go way back. Plus, that's my son's mother. We cool like that."

"Man, I don't give a damn how long you've been knowing her. That's *my* woman and this is *my* house. Don't let it happen again."

8

John Henry stood up. "Or what? You gonna beat me down, Raymond? Huh? What you gonna do, man?"

Raymond stood his ground. "Let's just say we'll handle it like men."

John Henry threw his head back and laughed.

"I'mah let that threat go this time."

Sheba stepped in the middle of them like she always did. "John Henry. You're wrecking the mood in here."

"Fine. I apologize for my *inappropriateness*. Is that better?"

Raymond had had enough. "Man—I ain't got time for this foolish ish. Sheba, I'm going downstairs until your company leaves."

As soon as he was gone Sheba snapped her head around to John Henry.

"Why are you always starting shit?"

"Raymond takes everything too serious. I was kidding around. No harm done."

"Kidding is for kids, John Henry. We're grown ass people."

"Okay, okay. Calm down. Can you make me a plate to go? And where's my son? You didn't tell him I was coming over?"

"Yeah, I told him. But he has late practice tonight."

"Tell him to call his old man when he gets in. I'm out."

She nodded, got up and walked him to the door. On the way back down the hall she paused in front of a floor length mirror to appreciate what God had given her at birth.

Sheba had that Tyra Banks kind of beauty. She had front *and* back working on her behalf. Her huge mane of hair was a dusty brown with hints of blonde. She had eyes like a leopard and skin the color of high grade amber. At thirty-nine, she could still cause a fender bender or two by simply walking down the street.

Sheba had never really been in love—not the way squares did it—flowers, cards, cooing and breathing on the phone all hours of the night. Sheba was in love with what men did for her, how she felt on their arm. If women didn't hate on her when she walked in the room with a man, she lost interest in a matter of days, sometimes hours.

When her and John Henry split up, not only had her heart been shattered, Sheba's entire operation walked out with him. She was depressed as hell, felt like giving up on life all together. Ronnie—short for Veronica—helped her get back on track.

Ronnie was an ex-cop who Sheba had bedded for about six months when she first broke it off with John Henry.

10

Ronnie was one of those androgynous women who could pass for a man in the right clothes and shoes. Ronnie used to be a wolf but life had turned her into one of the sheep. Well, more like a lamb…

Ronnie had a decade on the police department when she was shot in the line of duty. A few weeks out of rehab she got assigned to a cushy desk job. After five years of pushing paper, Ronnie negotiated an early retirement package and exited the war zone for good. She started a small consulting firm that provided security to business tycoons and B-list celebrities. That was how she met Sheba.

Sheba and Ronnie had set sail aboard one of those humungous cruise ships. Six days into their voyage across the Caribbean, Sheba emerged from the darkness knowing exactly what she had to do.

She had to start over. Rebuild her clientele. Recruit and hire a street team. Get a trusted source to keep her product flowing. It would take time but she eventually got it all back. Ronnie had been key in Sheba relaunching her empire.

Sheba liked that fact that Ronnie was licensed to pop a cap in somebody's ass if they stepped wrong. She liked it so much she brought Ronnie on to head up security at her new company *Ransome Industries*. Ronnie's connections in law enforcement provided important intel that helped keep the cops out of Sheba's illegal activities. Ronnie knew who on the force could be bought and what their price was. Sheba was happy to pay.

Sheba was smitten with John Henry but there was only one man on the planet who she would give her soul to the devil for. He was twenty-two, had dark curly hair and shoulders like a linebacker. That man was Diondre Jonathan Ransome, her son and one and only descendent.

Sheba would do anything for her *Dee-dee* but she couldn't let him know that. She had to keep him tough and his skin thick. She knew if she made life too easy he'd turn into a sheep and get slaughtered by the wolves.

Sheba's other job was keeping the peace between the man she used to love and the man she was in love with now. Her old life with John Henry had been dysfunctional and crazy, sexy and exciting. But life with John Henry always led to pain and disappointment.

Raymond was everything Sheba wanted in a mate. He was loving and thoughtful, smart and business minded. He was a great communicator and knew how to quiet her fire when necessary. He was also a beast in the bedroom that wouldn't quit until she was screaming his name. And her son Diondre adored him.

Between running her thiefdom, helping Dee-dee get through college and keeping her menfolk happy, Sheba's plate was always full. She'd be lying if she said she didn't have any feelings for John Henry. There was a time when he was the center of her world. They'd made plans to build an empire— one she planned on being the Queen of.

Sometimes she wondered how things would've turned out if she'd hung in there with John Henry. But life with Raymond was way too good to ever risk living on the edge of insanity again. Truth be told, there were days she kind of missed the crazy...

Two

Sheba yawned as he entered her. Shattered the last fragments of masculinity he'd held onto loving a woman like her.

Raymond withdrew and asked, "Am I boring you?"

"What? No, I just...I didn't sleep too well last night."

It cut him deep that her mind seemed to be so far away from their bed, so distant from the sacred act they were engaged in. He swallowed his tears, put his manhood out front and pushed the pain to a place where he couldn't feel it.

"Turn over on your stomach."

The corners of her lips turned upward into a devilish grin. She liked it when he got angry. She provoked him further. Forced him to the place where his rage lived.

"Turn over for what?"

He realized she was teasing him. She wanted to be punished. Raymond decided to play along with her little game.

"What's with all the questions? Turn over on your damn stomach and open your legs."

Sheba zeroed in for the kill. She turned over in slow motion, let him savor every curve and fold of her tight body.

"If you want this pussy, take it. Either take it or get your shit and leave."

He slapped her smooth ass a couple of times, gripped her hips, slid into her fast and withdrew slow. "You know whose pussy this is."

Jolts of pleasure rocked her body each time he slid in and out of her hotness. She moaned, hiked her ass up, spread her legs and took all he had to give.

"God, that's good. You feel....so damn good, Raymond."

She opened a little wider, antagonized him with further insults to his manhood. "You can't handle this pussy. Stop acting like a boy and be a man. I hate weak ass men. A weak ass man can't do nothing for me."

He slapped her ass again. Made her skin sting and sing simultaneously.

He was inside of her now, had her right where he wanted her. He pulled it all the way out and slid it back in with one smooth motion. Did that over and over until she was whimpering with pain and satisfaction.

She felt an orgasm building. Her middle finger went to her swollen pearl. He smacked her hand away. "That belongs to me. You touch it when I say you can."

"Please, baby....I need it...need to...."

He reached under their bodies and massaged her pearl like she liked it. Rode her strong and smooth while he squeezed and tickled it. He felt her walls gripping him. With

15

that perfect ass of hers high in the air, he watched the passion possess her—watched his magic take her to a place where she had no control.

"Oh shit....Raymond. I'm about to...I'm coming...coming for you."

He felt his organ swelling, the pace of his heart quickening.

"I'm the king of this castle. Don't forget it. Don't...ever...forget...."

"Fuck me, Raymond. Fuck me like I need to be fucked!"

She screamed as her body convulsed and the juices flowed like rivers.

Raymond threw his head back and moaned as his own orgasm ripped through his body.

Sex with Sheba was amazing. So amazing Raymond almost forgot that the woman he loved, the woman he would kill or die for, regularly allowed her ex to disrespect him.

Raymond had done everything a man was supposed to do and then some. He'd stepped up and raised Diondre like he was his. He'd given her the money to restart her company, *Ransome Industries*. But no matter what he did for Sheba, no matter how much of his soul he surrendered, she refused to let that crook in wolf's clothing leave their lives.

Raymond had grown tired of dealing with Sheba and John Henry's incestuous relationship. If things didn't change, he'd have to make some hard decisions. But not that day. Not that moment. Right then their love was as sweet as ripe fruit picked from the vine. And all he wanted to do was eat until he was full...

Three

It was seven a.m. in the Ransom Palace. The *Rawmeister*—Sheba's gourmet chef—was in the kitchen making breakfast.

Sheba sipped on her regular—a high protein smoothie filled with fruit and veggies. Diondre and Raymond had a bonified soul food breakfast with grits, turkey sausage, eggs with cheese and fresh squeezed OJ. Diondre was heading out to the carport to go to school when Sheba called him into her office.

"Whassup, ma? Running late for practice."

"Boy, don't rush me. I'll write you a note if you're late."

"Uh—don't you think I'm a little old for you to be writing me a note?"

"I didn't mean it like that. I meant I could get you a phony doctor's note or something."

"Ma, I'm in college. I write my own notes. Anyway, what's going on?"

"Tonight is Raymond's birthday and I want to take him out to a nice dinner. You got any ideas?"

"Yeah, it's called yelp.com and they have every restaurant known to man. I gotta go, Mom. What time y'all eating?

"What time *y'all* eating? What kind of foul language is that? I pay fifty thousand dollars a year for you to go to the one of the best colleges in the state and that's how you talk?"

"Mom, come on. Told you I'm in a hurry."

"Fine. Six o'clock. We'll go to *Versailles,* that Cuban restaurant on Venice Blvd."

"I'm there. Love you, Mama." He pecked her on the cheek, broke her icy persona for a minute or two.

"Love you too, Dee-dee. Stay out of trouble, son. You hear me?"

"Yes Ma'am."

Raymond came sauntering in the room with his long feet.

"Hey man, you got a game on Thursday?"
"Yeah, seven o'clock. You coming?"

"Yeah. Gonna try to bring your mom with me if I can get her out of the office for longer than five minutes."

"Good luck with that." They both chuckled, bumped fists and nodded in agreement. Diondre asked him, "Isn't it your birthday or something?"

"Yeah, I guess it is."

"Happy Birthday, Ray. Got mad love for you, man."

They hugged, did another manshake and Diondre scooted on out the door.

Sheba greeted Raymond by sitting on his lap and planting light kisses on his lips and face.

"Happy Birthday, Raymond."

"No big deal. Just another day."

"It *is* a big deal. Mama told me we should celebrate every birthday like it's the last. Because you never know, it might just be. Plus, I have a couple of gifts for you."

"What I want for my birthday I can't have."

"Anything. You name it and I'll buy it for you."

"What I want can't be bought. It's you. All of you. Minus John Henry."

"Don't start, Raymond. John Henry is Diondre's father and that's the only reason he's still in our lives."

"That's bullshit and you know it. He doesn't do shit for his son but buy him crap he doesn't need. Barely ever shows up for school functions. Flakes on his daddy son days. John Henry comes around here for you."

"Ray, you know I…"

"Let's just drop it. I'm not in the mood to be pissed off today."

"Yeah, let's." Sheba said getting up and heading to the kitchen. Raymond trailed closely on her heels.

Her cell phone rang. When she saw the caller ID she tried to reject the call before Raymond walked up. She was a hair too late.

Raymond peered over her shoulder at the screen.

"That's what I'm talking about. Why is this man calling you at eight o'clock in the morning?"

"I don't know. Maybe it has something to do with Diondre's college exams."

"And I'm having lunch with Jay-z. Don't insult my intelligence, Sheba."

She tried to change the subject. "The Changebringer is coming over to give you a massage."

Raymond knew she was sending John Henry a text message telling him she couldn't talk right then.

"Tell that man to stop calling my woman every five minutes. I'm tired of talking about this. Diondre's old enough to go and see his father where he lives if they want to spend time together."

She ignored his resentful words. "Look in the bathroom. That'll get rid of any doubt about where my heart is."

Raymond dipped down the hall, through their massive bedroom, to their designer bathroom that could've doubled as a studio apartment.

Sheba had candles burning everywhere. Soft jazz playing in the background. A Cuban cigar lay unlit in a marble ashtray waiting for Raymond to take a toke.

She walked in behind him with a plate of strawberries drizzled with chocolate.

"You're the only man I want and the only man I need Raymond Ogletree."

She reached around to his belt buckle and unsnapped his pants. Let them fall to the floor with a clank. With her right hand, she reached into his shorts and massaged his Johnson until it came to life. When he started moaning, she reached down and picked up an offering from the fruit plate. She fed him with her right hand while she worked his love stick with her left. Took him to level one.

"Fuckkkk...got damn, Sheba...slow down baby...."

She stopped the pleasure abruptly. Had him bent over in pain. His stiff stick was throbbing, bouncing like a ball on his leg.
She giggled and told him, "That's enough for now. In the water, mister."

"Why're you torturing me?"

He slid his body down into the steaming water, leaned his head back and relaxed. Sheba fed him another strawberry while she undressed.

Minutes later, Sheba and her plate of magic strawberries joined Raymond in the spacious tub. She straddled him and fed. Used her mouth to clean the chocolate off his face and her fingers. She set the plate down on the side of the tub, took a strawberry in her mouth and made him come and get it. Chocolate strawberry juice ran down her chest to her breasts. Raymond lapped it up like a pro.

He stared into her eyes like she was God.

"Why you put me through so much hell? Then you do shit like this? Spoil me. Feed me like I'm a king. I don't get it."

She inched up and slid her cave down onto his love then leaned forward and crushed her breasts against his chest.

"Because I'm that bitch, okay? Time for level 2." She said rocking her Yoni back and forth against his Johnson.

"Fuck….that feels good."

"Like. I. Said. Only you, Raymond."

"Your pussy is…so wet, baby. Awww shit……damn baby. Ride that dick. Just like….just like that."

Her breasts slapped him on the chin while she rode him like a stallion.

He lifted one of her plump mounds and brought it to his mouth. He flicked his tongue back and forth against her dark cherries until she was writhing. Raymond knew what took Sheba to her infinity. He sucked while she rode. Took the pressure from hard to soft. Licking, sucking, pulling on her nipple. She went crazy.

"You got me....so horny for this dick, Raymond. This is my dick. I love it....want it....my dick, got damnit!"

Raymond felt the back of Sheba's cave on the tip of his Johnson. He stayed still and let her ride down on it until he was there.

"Daddy can't take no more....I'm at level 3. Gonna pop...if you don't slow....down."

Sheba was gone, in another zone, her breathing erratic and intense.

"Come with me, Raymond. Fucking come with me right damn now."

"Let's....Come...Together. For my birthday."

They splashed and bounced until the tub was damn near empty and Sheba was screaming Raymond's name again and again.

They were drying each other off, sipping Champagne and chomping on more strawberries. Fully lit by the energy exchange they'd just shared. Raymond decided to be spontaneous and do something that had been on his mind for a while.

He went to the bedroom and came back with a small black box. He opened the box, took a fat diamond ring out and placed it on the palm of his hand. He walked up behind Sheba, tapped her on the shoulder and went down on his right knee. Sheba spun around so fast she almost fell onto him. When she realized what was in his hand and what he was doing, she started laughing like a hyena.

"Ray, what the hell are you doing?"

"I want you to marry me. I want to be your husband. I want you to be my wife. What we have is good. Real good. Let's do it. For life."

"You….you're serious? You're kidding right? I mean…shit like this—I don't know if marriage works for people like me. My mother said marriage takes the passion out of a relationship and turns it into obligation."

"With all due respect to Mamadee, your Mother was lacking in the relationship department. I'm trying to make a life with you and Deedee. I want to take care of you, love and provide for you. I'm making the ultimate commitment. What's your answer, Sheba?"

"I love you, Ray. I really do. But I….I can't answer right now. But I'm not trying to be anywhere but with you. Can you give me a little time?"

"Okay. I can do that. But I need you wear that ring for me."

"Put it on my finger."

After he slid the ring on her finger, he got up off his knee and kissed her. Kissed her deep enough to hide the fact that his heart was broken and bleeding all over the floor....

Four

As Raymond slid that beautiful diamond ring onto her finger Sheba heard her mother's voice saying: *Sometimes you gotta kill the wolves to keep the sheep alive.*

Sheba had watched her mother kill. Watched her murder the souls of hundreds of men who were gullible enough to believe she gave a damn about them. They arrived as wolves and left as slaughtered sheep. Pockets empty, hearts broken— the men were defenseless against her mother's calculating fangs.

Dorothy Ransome recruited her victims from country clubs and executive circles. She scoured obituaries for surviving spouses still in the thick of grieving women who'd actually loved them. Miss Dorothy's men had hedge funds and stock portfolios. They were world renowned ministers and history-making lawyers. No man was too high or too corrupt for Do-re-mi—that was her *game name*—to take them to the wash house.

Hot comb in hand, Miss Dorothy would sit Sheba on a high stool and teach her the *Wolf Philosophy* that would one day be her guiding force.

"I know it doesn't seem like it but we're the sheep, baby. These men we're scamming are the descendants of wolves who raped and lynched our ancestors. We built their cities and grew their crops. Their babies got big and strong off our grandmother's breast milk while our children starved. This here—what we're doing— is reparations, Bethsheba. Don't you ever forget it. We're just taking what's due to us."

At first, Sheba objected to the way her Mother treated what she saw as innocent people. As she got older, she started to understand that some of her Mother's victims weren't as innocent as she thought. A lot of them were takers, users of people. They came with selfish intentions and some of them didn't care who they had to take advantage of to get what they wanted. They saw her Mother as a means to an end—so her Mother treated them accordingly.

Sheba had always given John Henry the credit for making her who she was but Dorothy's role in her evolution couldn't be denied. It was her Mother who convinced her people were dispensable, that all of them were pawns in the game of life.

While Raymond took a nap, Sheba went downstairs to the exercise room and called John Henry. He answered on the first ring which meant he wanted something.

"What's up, John Henry? Why you call me at the crack of dawn? You know it pisses Raymond off."

"Fuck his weak ass. All sensitive and shit. My son lives there. I should be able to call anytime I want."

Sheba didn't have time for his drama. "What's going on? What's so urgent?"

"I have an opportunity I wanna talk to you about."

"How much does it cost?"

"You know what--forget it. You always got something negative to say. That's the shit that broke us up."

Seething with anger at the gall of him to blame her for their marriage failing Sheba corrected the record, "What broke us up, John Henry, was you going behind my back to my connect. What broke us up was you selling the same product I was carrying at a cheaper cost. What broke us up was you screwing my assistant to get intel on my operation and then waiting until the last minute to tell me I was under surveillance. Let's keep it one hundred and we won't have any problems."

"Why're you always bringing up the past, Sheba?"

Sheba knew the fact that he hadn't cussed her out and hung up the phone meant that he really needed something.

Curiosity got the best of her. She exhaled, released the anger and asked, "So, tell me about your opportunity."

She imagined him sitting on the terrace off the bedroom at his estate, cell phone to his ear, wearing a white wife-beater and silk boxers, shoulders wide and pecks hard. She picked up a ten-pound weight and did a few curls while she listened.

"Me and my boy Vic. We got this business opportunity. All we need is one more wolf to help us pull it off and a little bit of investment capital. A loan."

"Details."

"We go to the casino, hit the roulette wheel, put money on every number. Big payoff if we can make it pop."

"How much up front money we talking?"

29

"Around twenty grand if we do it right."

Sheba started adding the pluses and minuses. "That's a lot of cheddar. Cameras and stuff in the casino make the risk high."

"Come on, Sheba. This is a sure thing."

It made her feel good to hear John Henry beg. She thought about toying with him but thought better. His idea was a good one but it was way too much risk for her.

"Find another investor. I'm gonna pass on this one."

"We just need a seat warmer. We're in there two hours max and we're out."

"You talking about *me* going in there? Hell no. I'd never put my face on the front line. I'm a mother and a business woman. I have a son in college."

"You can slang that thang for a stranger but you can't help your baby's daddy come up?"

"Like I said, I'm an investor not a sales person."

"I was gonna use the take to pay for Dee-dee's college tuition."

"I have Dee-dee covered. Don't worry about that. I gotta run, John Henry. Heavy schedule today and…."

"Go to hell, Sheba. I made you. You were the daughter of a two-bit madam. I took you in and taught you the game. After all these years I come to you for help and this is how you act? Whatever. Lose my number. Tell Dee-dee he knows where to find his father if he wants to see me."

"I was wondering when the real John Henry Carter would step up. Kiss the crack of my ass." She told him before slamming the phone down.

Sheba went upstairs to the bedroom where Raymond was rubbing his body down with a woody-smelling lotion. She thanked God for giving her a sane man. He had a plush blue towel wrapped around his waist. She kissed his lips a few times before dropping to her knees.

"Bet you thought your birthday celebration was over. I'm just getting started old man."

"Old? Thirty-four isn't old."

She shut him up by sliding his Johnson between her lips. She let her tongue mingle with his sweetness. She took in as much of it as she could without choking. Did a viper-like move at the base of the head. Felt that vine harden and swell. Pulled her head back and worked the tip until he grabbed the sides of her face.

"Slow down, Sheba. You got....got me at level two already. I wanna savor this ride."
She licked and talked. "Love, love, love the way you taste. Feed me, baby. Feed me until I can't eat any more...."

"Level three, baby. Slow downnnnnn. Shit..."

She worked her magic slow then fast. It wasn't long before he was calling uncle.

"Level four, Sheba. Can't stop. Fuck….I'm coming….coming for you again."

Five

Sheba nodded to security as she made her way down the polished hallway, past an original collection of art by *Louise Mcgaw* to a state-of-the-art conference room where her team was waiting. Ronnie and the rest of the group rose from their seats as Sheba entered the boardroom. When she was seated, they followed suit. She didn't bother greeting them—just jumped into the business of the day.

"The second quarter profit report for *Ransome 2K* looks good. I'm gonna need our Team Leads to do a check on your reps and make sure they're following protocol. We've kept our street cred solid and avoided run-ins with powers that be. If we keep it strong there'll be some fat bonuses at the end of the month. Any questions?"

Everybody nodded their understanding.

"Great. Get out there and keep that green flowing. Power up!"

"Power-up!" The team answered in unison.

"Ronnie, I need to talk with you. Meet me in my office in fifteen."

"Sure thing, boss lady."

When Sheba got to her office she saw a young man with skin the color of bark sitting in the reception area. He reminded her of the Hip Hop, R&B sensation, *Usher*. He looked familiar but Sheba couldn't place his face. She looked over at Ronnie for the intel she was seeking.

"That's Fabian Mcknight. Says he's a friend of Diondre's. Looking for work."

"Little Fabian? Haven't seen him in years. Thought he and his family moved to Detroit. Have him come on in."

A few shakes later, Diondre's high school buddy was sitting in the massive office that Sheba occupied at *Ransome 2K*. His eyes took in the Italian leather couches, Peruvian rugs, full bar and coffee station like a hungry child. After he guzzled two cups of her gourmet java, Sheba introduced him to Ronnie and found out why he was there.

"Dang, Miss Ransome. Y'all balling out of control over here. Me and my moms just got back to Cali. I'm looking for work. You remember me don't you?"

"Of course I remember you. I darn near raised you. You've grown up so much I didn't recognize you at first. What kind of job you looking for?"

"The kind that pays long paper."
"What kind of skills you have?"

"Little of this and a little of that. But my specialty is working with all types of people."

Sheba had a soft spot for Fabian but she also had a policy against hiring friends and family to work the line.

She chewed on the end of her pen for a minute then told him, "I have stuff you can do in the office. Doesn't pay that much but its steady income, great bennies and a way-cool place to work."

"Thanks, Miss Ransome. I appreciate the opportunity. But I'm really in need of some long chips right now. I don't mind getting my hands dirty for the right opportunity."

Sheba was quiet for a few minutes. Ronnie watched her weigh the pros and cons of hiring Fabian like the alpha wolf she was.

"Email your resume and contact info to Ronnie and we'll call you." Sheba stood up to dismiss him. "I'll let Dee-dee know you came by."

"So I got the job?"

Ronnie stepped up to close the meeting and cut the conversation short. "We'll be in touch. Thanks for coming by."

"Let my frat brother know I'mah roll through as soon as we get settled in."

After he was gone, Ronnie queried her boss on hiring Fabian.

"You aren't gonna hire Dee-dee's friend are you?"

"As you know, my policy is to never put friends or family on the street team. But Fabian's a smart kid. And I need somebody I can trust, somebody that'll give me the inside scoop. I might have to make an exception this one time."

"I've seen that kid somewhere before. Think he was in a rehab for crystal meth. You really thinking about bringing him on board?"

"I'm glad he got some help for his problem. This is business, Ronnie. If he had the nerve to come in here and stand up for himself, I gotta give him a chance. Plus, he's family. I damn near raised that boy."

"More reason not to hire him."

Ronnie rarely bucked Sheba's decisions. They both knew she was taking a big chance by voicing her opinion on Sheba's choice.

"That boy doesn't have the heart for street work. He's hard on the outside and all gooey on the inside. You put him out there and the streets are gonna turn him into a lamb, skin em' and cook him up for dinner. He's gonna end up dead or in jail. And it ain't gonna take that long either."

"I appreciate you giving me your unsolicited professional opinion but I think he can handle it."

Ronnie stood up. "You're making a mistake, Sheba. Dee-dee's gonna…"

"Conversation is *over*. Do the background check, make sure there's nothing serious on his rap sheet, get his paper work going. In the meantime, I need you to have a seat. There's something I have to talk to you about."

Ronnie semi-rolled her eyes and sat back down.

"Did you get that information I asked you for? About Rebecca, the girl Diondre's been seeing?

"Yep, she's clean as a whistle. Not even a jaywalking ticket. Anything else?"

"Damn. Dee-dee sure can pick 'em huh?"

"Yep. He did good this time. Real glad he picked a normie and not some money hungry con artist."

"Ronnie, what's going with you? You seem a little uptight."

Ronnie looked down at the floor for a minute then told her, "I met somebody. Somebody nice. She ain't no Rebecca but she's a good woman. She doesn't like the line of work I'm in. I'm thinking about taking a break."

"You better tell her to get with the program. Anybody that comes into your life trying to run it is a problem."

"It's not like that. She...she cares about me."

"You said you just met her. How can you be so sure?"

"Look, I gotta go. Computer guy's coming in to set up our new system."

Ronnie headed for the door.
"Ronnie."

"Yeah, Boss Lady?"

"I'm happy you met somebody."

Sheba saw the corners of Ronnie's mouth turn up into a smile.

"But don't quit your job over some punanny."

Ronnie chuckled and said, "Thanks, boss lady. I ain't trying to go nowhere. Not yet anyway. You have a good night."

Sheba picked up the phone to start returning business calls but before she could punch in the first number, she heard his voice and her hand froze in motion.

She found her center just in time to see John Henry walking toward her office. He had on a wine-colored suit with a stark white shirt. A Cuban brim tilted to the right on his apple-shaped head made him look exotic and sexy. As usual, John Henry had an entourage of women from *Ransome 2K* following him down the hall, feigning over him, cooing and lusting.

"Thanks, ladies. I can handle it from here."

He tipped his hat to Ronnie before dipping into Sheba's office.

When he sat down Sheba got a whiff of his aftershave. An enticing combination of jasmine and musk. Bastard loved to tease her with his fineness.

"To what do I owe the gift of one of your rare visits. And how come you didn't call? I could've been in meetings."

"Just wanted you to tell you that you shouldn't've slept on that investment opp I offered you. Somebody stepped up and we made that shit pop."

"Congrats. I'm happy for you. But I've got work to do and I don't have time to chat."

"You can't take a few minutes for an old friend?"

Her phone vibrated with a text. It was Ronnie making sure she didn't need a John Henry intervention. She sent her a text back letting her know she was okay.

"Can you do that shit on your own time? I'm here to talk to you about our son."

"In case you didn't notice, I'm at work, John Henry. You can't just barge in here and expect me to drop everything. It wouldn't have killed you to call before coming. We could've talked over lunch."

"I'm your son's father. Nothing or no one is more important than our boy."

"What is it you want to talk about that couldn't wait?"

"I want Dee-dee to live with me for a few months. I feel like we're drifting and I think it would be good for him."

39

"That would be a good thing if it weren't for that fact that you have all kinds of illegal shit going down at your crib. Not to mention the whores that run in and out of your house like it's a barn yard."

"I keep business separate from family. You know that."

"Dee-dee's in college and he needs a quiet, stable place to live. When you clean it up we can talk about him living with you. Until then, he's good right where he is."

"That's my son too, Sheba. You got that nigga Raymond all up and through his life but I'm not good enough?"

"Is that what this about, John Henry?"

He got up, walked over to her chair and got down on his knees. The smell of his manly body slithered up her nose and damn near hypnotized her.

"Diondre needs both his parents. I'm Dee-dee's father. It ain't right that Raymond gets more quality time with my son than I do."

"You can see your son whenever you want. I've never gotten in the way of you spending time with Dee-dee. Half the time you don't even show up and don't even have the courtesy to call. You have Dee-dee waiting and wondering if something happened to you."

He ignored her comments and kept flirting. "I miss you, She. We're supposed to be together, raising our son, building our dynasty. We never should've split up."

He leaned into her, put his thick, succulent lips on her neck. She felt his big stick on her knee. Thick and solid. Her kitty was working up on a soft purr. And when her pussy cat spoke she was doomed to obey its commands. She had to act fast to avoid a travesty.

"Back up off of me, John Henry. You know I'm with Raymond now. You shitted on what we had. Not once but three times. In the end you destroyed everything I worked my whole life to build. How could I ever trust you again?"

"How you gonna blame me for what happened? That was karma, baby. We make our money off the devil's handiwork. Ain't my fault he called your marker in. Sometimes things happen to protect us from something worse."

"I'm done talking about this. I need you to get up and out of my office. I have somewhere to be and I have to finish what I'm working on before I leave."

He put his hand on her face. "Eleven years, Sheba. That's how much time we put in. How you gonna throw that away?"

Just when the nightmare seemed like it couldn't get any worse, her intercom buzzed. Security informed her that Raymond was making her way toward her office.

"You gotta get out of here, John Henry. Now. Leave. Please, if you care about me at all, go."

Suddenly it dawned on her that John Henry had set her up. He'd always had a memory like an elephant. He knew it was Raymond's birthday.

Sneaky bastard.

He figured she and Ray would meet at the office for whatever they had planned. He wanted Raymond to catch them in an embrace or maybe even in the middle of foreplay.

John Henry grabbed her around the waist, pulled her to him and kissed her on the cheek.

"Get off me, John Henry! Stop! I told you...."

Raymond rounded the corner just as she pushed him off of her.

Six

"What the fuck? Man, if you don't get your hands off my woman...."

Raymond charged toward John Henry like a bull coming out of a pen.

Sheba's heart went into overdrive as John Henry slid his blazer back to reveal the pearl handle of a custom-made pistol. When he slid it out of the holster, Sheba jumped in front of Raymond.

Raymond threw his hands in the air like he was at a bank robbery. John Henry stood there staring at him, bouncing the gun on his muscular thigh, finger on the trigger. Raymond slowly lowered his arms but kept them in plain sight.

Raymond counter challenged John Henry. "What you gonna do, man? Unlike you, I'm not scared to die for what I love. Either shoot me or get the fuck out of here."

If Sheba didn't intervene, two rams were going to war in the middle of her office.

"That's enough! Don't forget this is my place of business."

They stared each other down, each man daring the other to make a move.

Sheba was relieved when John Henry put the gun back in the holster, closed and buttoned his jacket. Raymond's blood cooled off ten or fifteen degrees.

Raymond walked over to Sheba and put his arm around her. "This is *my* woman. What y'all had is over. Done. Check the expiration date, broh. She's not coming back."

"I came by to talk to my son's mother. Didn't know I needed permission. Tell Dee-dee to call me, She. I'm out."

John Henry knew Raymond hated it when he called her *She*. *She* was the nickname he used when they were a couple.

"Get the fuck out of here, man," Raymond told him stepping in front of Sheba.

John Henry blew Sheba kiss, tipped his hat at Raymond and dipped on out of the door.

When he was gone and the wind had cooled, Sheba started packing up her briefcase.

"Told you to get his ass in check. I'm sick of this shit, Sheba."

"He showed up unannounced. Called me this morning about investing in a business deal. I turned him down cold. He came by to gloat. Apparently, he found another investor and they made it rain. Guess he wanted to rub it in my face."

Raymond brushed his hand over his head. "I need some air. You ready to go?"

"Not gonna let his foolishness mess up your birthday."

"All I need is a drink, a fat cigar and some Cuban food and I'll be great. Maybe dance a couple songs to some of that Mariachi music. That and some of that juicy juice you gave me this morning and we good."

That made her smile.

"You're so greedy. Come on birthday, boy. Let's go party."

Seven

Dinner was spectacular. *Versaille's* Cuban chicken, black beans, rice and sweet plantains made the birthday boy gleam. Sheba kept the Tequila coming. Forty-five minutes later, Raymond had forgotten all about John Henry's arms being wrapped around his woman in the middle of the afternoon.

Diondre arrived with a surprise for his stepfather. He and Sheba had been working on it for months. It had been no easy feat keeping Raymond in the dark. Raymond guarded the *Ransome* palace like a soldier.

Sheba and Diondre had flown to London for a rare auction of A-list celebrity memorabilia. It'd cost them a grip but when all was said and done they had outbid a record label exec, a rock and roll museum and a movie star to take home the prize.

Diondre put the box down in front of Raymond and laid it against his knees. Sheba whipped out her phone so she could record the moment Raymond laid his eyes on it.

"This is one big ass box. Y'all went to too much trouble for an old man."

"Shut-up and open the box, Raymond." Sheba was so excited she could hardly contain herself.

Raymond's lips turned up in a huge smile when he saw what it was.

"Is this what I think it is?"

"Look at the authentication papers." Diondre told him proudly.

"This guitar belonged to…Jimi Hendrix! It's a *Fender*. How in the hell you guys get this?"

Before they could answer, one of the band members invited Raymond to the stage. Sheba loved it when her plans came off with perfection. Raymond made his way to the center of the room with his new friend in tote. The band leader connected Raymond's shoulder strap to the guitar, slung it over his shoulder and plugged it into the amp.

Raymond stood there for a minute, shaking his head in disbelief. Finally, he pulled the microphone to him and said a few words.

"My lady and my….son…they got this ax for my birthday. It once belonged to a legendary string man. The one and the only, Jimi Hendrix. This…this is something a man like me never dreamed of holding in his hands. To get to play it….man….yeah…let's crank this thing up and get it popping up in here!"

People in the restaurant started cheering. Sheba pulled a chair up in front of the stage so she could get it all on film.

The drummer played the first licks of Hendrix's hit song, *Hey Joe* then segued into *Machine Gun* and closed out with *Purple Haze*.

When they got to the third song, Raymond was slamming his fingers across the strings like a pro while the patrons in the restaurant danced and cheered him on.

Sheba and Diondre stood and clapped for Raymond as he made his way back to the table.

"Sheba…Dee-dee…that was…man—that was another world kind of birthday present. Thank you. Thank both of you."

After dinner they waited for the valet to bring their pearl white Daimler around. Raymond kept rubbing his hands over the guitar, petting it like a kitten.

He pulled Diondre to him for a manly hug. "Love you, boy. You know that, right?"

"Love you too, Dad."

Raymond got quiet. Sheba got quiet too. Diondre had never called Raymond dad before. They both knew if John Henry ever heard Diondre address him that way….

Raymond decided to nip it in the bud.

"Man…you know your father wouldn't appreciate you calling me that. I love you like you're my own flesh. Always will. But call me Raymond so we can keep the peash."

"You mean peace don't you?" Sheba chuckled.

"He knows what I mean." Raymond said slurring his words.

Diondre still wasn't letting up.

"You've been more of a dad to me than he ever has and probably ever will be."

Sheba was relieved when the valet pulled up with their vehicle. This night was getting as deep as one of those backwoods swamps in Alabama. Raymond was stupid drunk. Diondre seemed like he'd gotten caught up in the moment. It was a perfect combination for a full-on blow out. Sheba figured she'd cut the convo short and get things straightened out in the morning. Diondre wasn't having it.

"I'm right ain't I, Ma? Daddy's just the man who gave you his seed."
"Let's talk about it another time, son."

Raymond stumbled over to the passenger side of the car. He stuttered his response over a mist of foul Tequila breath. "Sheba….when you gon' stop being that man's doormat."

Diondre crawled into the back seat while Sheba tried to ignore Raymond's comment.

Sheba eased into the driver seat. "You're drunk, Ray. Let it go. We had a great dinner. You got a great gift. Go home and sleep it off. We'll talk later. Fasten your seat belt."

Raymond slurred, "Fuck…fuck it. Let's go home."

Raymond was asleep in the passenger seat ten minutes later.

49

Diondre leaned forward and told her, "He's right, Ma. Daddy just uses us. I'm not saying he doesn't love me but what Raymond has done for me—for us—for the last ten years…if Daddy was half the man Ray…"

"That's enough, son."

"I'm tired of kissing his ass."

"Watch your tone, Diondre. He's still your father and I'm still your mother. Don't mess this night up talking about something you don't know nothing about."

"I know my Daddy's been MIA for a long ass time. I know Raymond took care of us after Daddy did some foul mess that sabotaged your whole operation."

"Your Daddy loves you. That's all you need to know. He…he's been through a lot—more than your spoiled butt can understand."

"You're just making excuses for him. That nigga ain't…"

Sheba reached over the seat and backhanded Diondre in the mouth.

"Told you to watch your mouth! You wouldn't be here if it wasn't for your Daddy. You need to show him a little respect."

"Fuck him and fuck you! Let me the hell out of this car!"

Diondre grabbed the handle and tried to open the door.

"Dee-dee! No...wait! Cars are coming!"

Sheba slammed on the brakes so hard Dee-dee's cheek slammed against into the back of the seat. She saw a few drops of blood trickle down her son's lip.

Raymond woke up and looked around. "What's going on? Why is the car stopped? Dee-dee, why you yelling? Why is your mouth bleeding?"

Sheba looked at Dee-dee with tears in her eyes.

She silently begged him not to tell Raymond why they were arguing.

Diondre took pity on her. "Nothing. I just need some air."

"Let the man out, Sheba."

"I'll send the driver to pick you up, son."

"I can get home on my own."

Sheba hit the unlock button so he could get out.

Before he walked off, Diondre told her. "I hope you wake up before you lose the best thing that ever happened to us. I really do."

Sheba was about to let her inner wolf claw the side of his face with a few choice words but she realized her baby boy was right. Being cared for and loved by a man like Raymond had changed her life. John Henry had done nothing but take from her. He used her to build his empire. Then when she wouldn't give him what he wanted--which was for her to close her business and be his arm piece, he tried to destroy her.

But thankfully you can't take an alpha wolf down with one bite. He had wounded her. He left her on the road for dead. But she was Mamadee's daughter. She was a descendant of the alpha of all alpha wolfs. And because of the blood that flowed through her veins she bounced back even stronger than she was before.

Eight

Sheba was quiet the rest of the drive in. When she turned into the parking structure at Ransome Industries, she patted Raymond on his thigh a couple of times to wake him up.

"Ray, I need to run into the office and pick up some files. You mind?"

Raymond looked over at her. "You gonna tell me what you and Dee-dee were arguing about?"

"It's over. I prefer not to rehash it if it's alright with you."

"That means it was about that bastard. Whenever you don't wanna talk about something, it has to do with him."

"Drop it, Raymond. Let the night end in peace."

She parked in her reserved space.

"I'm coming with you. Need to drain the main bank."

Sheba was sitting at her desk flipping through paperwork when Raymond returned from the lavatory. He sat on the edge of the desk. Took her hand in his. She stood up, draped her arms across his shoulders and kissed him on the lips.

Raymond lifted her chin and told her, "You know I love you, right?"

"Yes, Raymond. I know you love me. You know I love you?"

"Sometimes. Sometimes I'm not sure. Feels like…like I'm your second choice."

"You think I couldn't be with him if I wanted to?"

"I think you do."

"You think I do what?"

"I think you *do* want to be with him. But you know how crazy he is."

"There was a time when I was addicted to John Henry's dysfunction but not anymore. Stop tripping off something that's nothing. I love you and that's all you need to know. Come here, birthday boy. I know what you need to relax."

She slid the files she came to pick up into her briefcase, stuck her I-phone on the charger and turned on some music. Some of that sexy, bad girl trap-style rap music crooned over the speakers.

Sheba took his hand and led him to the conference room adjacent to her office. She slid her backside onto the table, used her index finger to summon him to her.

When he was in front of her, she wisped her tongue across his lips, kissed his mouth the way she was getting ready to kiss his Johnson. She slid her hand down below, unzipped his pants, saw that stick was at full attention. She slithered off the table, switched places with him and put his backside on the table.

"Lay back." She commanded.

After he did what she told him, she bent over and sucked it into her mouth without the help of her hands. Did a Honey-Meets-Mr-Marcus move and made him jerk with pleasure.

"Mmmmm. Damn, you're a bad bitch."

In between slurps she said, "Stop...telling me...shit...I already know."

She sucked just the head of it between her lips, bobbed her head up and down and twisted the base like she was grinding pepper.

"You're *my* bad bitch."

"Like I said...."

When he was ripe she mounted him. She was surprised how wet she had gotten just from giving him head. Her body released an uncontrollable moan as he slid in to her.

"Oh God, Raymond. You're so fucking hard."

He reached out and massaged the pearl that had his name inscribed on it. His touch took her pleasure up another notch.

She started riding it. She knew he had ten, maybe fifteen good pumps before he exploded. She moved up and down nice and slow then leaned her body forward so his Johnson massaged her pearl while she rotated her hips.

"I….I'm about to come, Raymond. Shit…Fuck…Come with me…Got damnit…Oh shit…I'm fucking coming."

His thickness slid in and out of her until she felt his seeds explode between her walls. In the midst of her monster orgasm and his powerful climax, a revelation of epic proportions dawned on her.

She'd forgotten to put on a condom.

Nine

Sheba and Fabian—Diondre's brother from another mother—were at *Roscoe's Chicken and Waffles* having a bonified soul food lunch. Fabian ate like the refrigerator at home was on E. Like he didn't know when his next meal would happen.

"Danggggg, Fae. Slow down for a minute. You're gonna give yourself indigestion eating that fast."

He was embarrassed but that didn't stop him from chewing. "This food is good. I'mah have to get some of this to go."

He chomped, swallowed and ate some more. "I know....know you real busy. Trying to hurry up so you can get on with your day."

"I'm the boss remember? That means I set my own schedule. You can get another meal to-go if you want."

"Auight, Mrs. Ransome."

Sheba noticed that his lips were burned in the middle. She started to question him about it but realized it was probably from smoking weed.

"I want to talk to you about a position opening up in Venice Beach. It's a prime area and there's a lot of work down that way. But we need to be clear on a few things before I put you on payroll."

"Sure thing. I'm all ears."

"Typically I don't put family—and that's what you are to me and Dee-dee—on my street team. I also don't use newbies. But I'm making...."

"I can handle myself, Mrs. Ransome. I..."

"Don't interrupt me, Fabian."

"My bad."

"As I was I saying, I normally don't use newbies but I'm making an exception for you. But I need you to understand that this is a grown man's job. If you have a weak stomach, if your skin is thin, I can put you in an office gig and everything'll be copasetic."

"I can handle it. Just let me know what you need me to do."

She ran down the ins and outs of his drug peddling responsibilities. Talked to him about compensation and bennies. At the end of her little pep talk, she explained in detail, the health hazards of his j.o.b.

"It's important that you stay within our territory. There are Kingpins out there that don't take kindly to folks who try to move product in a no-fly zone. *Ransome Industries* has a twenty-block radius. We have real estate that doubles as a safe house if you get in a situation. Wisdom is the QPIC for your region. You have a problem, just pick up the phone and call her or get to one of the safe houses."

She handed him a card with a phone number.

"Got it. Stay in our territory. Call Wisdom or go to a safe house if I get in trouble. What's a QPIC?"

"Queen Pin in Charge. For the first ninety days, you'll shadow her and her peeps. You pass their tests, you get to fly solo. Understood?"

"Understood."

"Any other questions?"

"When I get paid?"

"You get paid when we get paid. Your collections go well, we give you a bonus. Typically, payroll comes out on Fridays."

"When I start?"

"Next week. I'm gonna need you to register for school. Everybody in my operation has a cover. School's yours. Take a couple of drama classes, a computer class, whatever. Also, we don't use our product. I don't care what you do on your off hours but your head needs to be clear when you're working for me."

"Got it. Cool. I guess me and Dee gonna be boys again. He know what you do for living?"

"Of course he does. But the details of your job description stay between us. You slip up and tell him something your contract is canceled. Have I made myself clear?"

"Yeah. I'm clear."

She peeled off ten c-notes and pulled out a chip-free cell phone.

"Here's a throw away cell phone and few chips to get yourself some proper gear.   Check in with Human Resources on Monday for your company car."

His eyes lit up when she put the money in his hand. "And remember, *keep the bling to a minimum.* You can have swag but don't overdo it. You start flashing ice and rocking grills, the po-po's are gonna start paying attention."

"I got this, Mrs. Ransome. I'm gonna make you proud. You'll see."

As Sheba walked toward the door she thought, *Ronnie's right. He's as green as the grass. Hope the streets don't eat him alive.*

Ten

They were at breakfast when she told Dee-dee about running into Fabian and giving him a job at *Ransome Industries*. They hadn't spoken since Raymond's birthday.

"What's crack-a-lacking son?"

"I'm good, Moms. You aught?"

Sheba knew her flesh and blood better than he knew himself. He was being cool but he hadn't totally forgiven her. Not yet.

"I'm cool. Your boy came by to see me the other day."

"Who?"

"Fabian."

"That jigga's back in Cali huh? Guess he was too soft for D-town. What he talking about?"

"Singing a sad song. Asked me for some help."

"Broh know he ain't cut out for these streets. He tries to act hard but I've seen him mitch up under pressure. You put him on a desk?"

Sheba lied. "Yeah. Told him I'll promote him if he proves himself."

"Thanks, Ma. I appreciate you looking out for him. Fay's my boy. One of the few real G's I can kick it with."

"I got you. Always have, always will."

"You and Raymond work out your misunderstanding?"

"Stay in your lane, son."

"Just asking."

"We're cool."

"That's good. He's a good man."
"I know that, Dee-dee. But John Henry is your father. Good, bad or ugly, he's the man who brought you in the world."

"That's *all* he did. Im jes' saying. There's more to being a father than getting a woman pregnant."

Sheba smiled to hide the sadness she felt over her son's pain about his absentee father. "My son spouting wisdom? Come give your mama a kiss."

He leaned over and kissed her on the cheek. "What? It's true."

"You're right, son. There *is* more to being a father than making a baby. But crazy as he is, he loves you."

"I love him too. Just tired of him lying to me."

"You talk to him about it?"

"What I'm gonna say? You know how Dad is. He'll just get mad and shut down."

She could hear the hurt in his words. Child just wanted to talk to his father but being a father hadn't ever been John Henry's priority.

"Don't give up on him."

"I was thinking about asking Raymond to adopt me."

Sheba's stomach did a flip when he said that. But she had to stay calm. If she reacted, it was over.

"That's sweet, son. It really is. But you know that would destroy your father."

"Bump him."

"You don't mean that."

"Yeah, I do."

The Rawmeister walked up and thankfully cut their talk short. After he took their plates away, Sheba pulled Diondre over to her and hugged him around his neck.
"Don't do anything drastic right now. I'm gonna talk to your Dad. Can you do that for me, son?"

"Yeah. Sure. It's not gonna do any good but I'll wait."

"Thanks, Dee-dee. Love you."

"Love you too, Ma. Like fried chicken and greens with hot water corn bread."

"Like oxtails, rice and gravy with Louisiana hot sauce." She told him kissing his brown forehead.

"Like homemade peach cobbler with vanilla ice cream." He answered.

"Like....hell, I can't think of anything else."

It was their game. They professed their love for one another according to their favorite soul foods.

But even in that sweet moment Sheba knew that if she didn't do something to make Dee-dee and John Henry see eye to eye, things were going to get bad. What she didn't know was just how bad they would get....

Sheba had to convince John Henry how important it was for him to step up and be the kind of father Diondre needed. If he continued to be a show-up-when-its-convenient daddy then maybe her seed *should* pick another father. But right then, all Sheba wanted was to be in a place called peace in paradise. Problem was, she was gonna have to travel through hell to get there...

Eleven

As much as Sheba wanted to hate John Henry, she couldn't. John Henry had been shaped and molded into the person he was. Born in a one-horse town called Baker about ninety-miles shy of the Las Vegas border, John Henry's parents were sharecroppers who picked and packed lettuce, bell peppers and onions for a living. That translated into them barely having enough food and money to survive. It was hard to raise a child when you didn't know how you were going to eat the next day.

John Henry Senior took a part time job as a card dealer for one of the smaller casinos at the State Line. Desperate for extra money, he started playing the penny slots on his off days. Penny bets turned into dollar wagers with way more losses than wins. A year later, without telling his wife, he turned over the deed to their home for a few thousand dollars. Unable to keep up with the payments to get their cottage out of hock, the family ended up with their belongings on a dirt road. After a short stint in a homeless shelter, John Henry Junior, his mother and father moved into a small RV in a sea of mobile homes right outside of Vegas. His father still wasn't finished wrecking their lives.

John Senior graduated into a full-fledged habitual gambler. He had a few good wins playing tournaments. By then he'd learned about the point system and took advantage of the comp rooms and free meals wherever he was playing. People mistook him for a high roller and started treating him like a baller. Then he hit another losing streak.

He borrowed money from a Loan Shark to clear up his marker at the casino. When he couldn't pay off the loan, the

Shark's henchmen came to the RV park and beat the crap out of him. Afraid for his life, John Senior bartered with the only possession he had left—his fifteen-year-old son.

John Henry junior dropped out of high school and became the assistant to the primary debt collector for the Mulligan Brothers Cartel. At six-feet tall, two hundred and eighteen pounds, John Henry junior's size was intimidating. As soon as people saw him coming through the door they paid whatever they owed. He was so good at getting debts paid off by the Cartel's clients they promoted him to lead collector.

Ultimately, John Henry junior became the right-hand man for the top guy. It was a prime position with great pay, exceptional benefits and high risk. Then the Mulligan Brothers were taken down by another cartel. Fortunately, they'd heard about John Henry's rep and wanted him to work for their operation.

They temporarily put him under a French-American mobster who ran drugs in Southern California. A few months later he was transferred back to the security detail.

Sadly, his father continued to gamble. John Henry spent most of his earnings paying off the debts his dad racked up. A year later, the cops found John Henry's father face down in a ditch with two bullets in his head.

John junior was sad about his father dying but when he thought about all the havoc he caused him and his Mother, he was relieved he was gone. He moved his mother to a nice little house in Henderson and gave her a monthly stipend. He took her on shopping trips up and down the strip and even bought her a mink coat which she never wore. A year later, his Mother started having trouble walking. Her ankles swelled to the size of cantaloupes. She lost her eyesight and then couldn't walk two or three steps without sitting down. Six months later she was gone.

After his mother passed, John Henry stopped eating. All he did was go to work, come home and cry himself to sleep. He was a ruthless, drug-dealer-turned-cartel-security who missed his mama so much he wanted to die. John Henry's mother was the only person in the world that he felt really cared about him. With both his mother and his father deceased, John Henry felt like a ship sailing across the ocean with no destination.

It was during this period that John Henry met Sheba. She was in Las Vegas on a vacay with a few college friends. He was at the *Wynn Hotel* doing a special detail for the Big Man when she and her girls sat down at the table to play roulette. Sheba kept staring at him and smiling. He found himself unable to take his eyes off her. She looked familiar but he couldn't place where he knew her from. The Big Man--that's what they called his new boss--noticed Sheba checking for John Henry and told him to introduce himself.

Sheba gave him her number and they started talking by phone. The Big Man was sent back East to head up a budding fraction. John Henry moved to Los Angeles and went to work full time for the French Mobster he'd worked for once before. He and Sheba started dating and in a matter of months, she became his entire world. A year later, she graduated from college and two months after that, they eloped to Jamaica and had a fairytale wedding.

Sheba's Mother was outraged when she found out her daughter had eloped. Sheba had been keeping John Henry away from her but now she had no choice but to introduce them. When he saw Miss Dorothy's face, he remembered when he'd met Sheba. Miss Dorothy was a good friend of the French Mobster they now called, The Godfather. Years before he and Sheba met, John Henry had accompanied The Godfather to Sheba's mother's house to handle some business.

Thankfully, Miss Dorothy—or Mamadee as she was affectionately called on the street, didn't remember him. He decided to let sleeping dogs lie. The less she knew about him the better. Little by little, Miss Dorothy warmed up. He started looking after her, dropping her a few coins and doing favors when she needed it. Favors like roughing up somebody who stepped wrong or did something she didn't particularly care for.

A few years later, early on a Sunday morning, Sheba called him hysterical. He was out on a job and had little privacy. In between her sobbing, John Henry heard her say that the maid had arrived to clean her Mother's house and found her unconscious. They pronounced Mamadee DOA at the local hospital. Her cause of death, a massive stroke.

Sheba coped with the grief of losing her mother by staying insanely busy. She volunteered at the hospital, raised money for the animal shelter and mentored kids at a local homeless program.

Sheba felt lost without her mama. She searched for something that would make her feel alive. Nothing seemed to work. A week later, she started throwing up every morning after breakfast. She thought she had a stomach virus. The doctor confirmed that she and John Henry were expecting a baby. Sheba was ecstatic. John Henry was ambivalent. After

Sheba gave birth to their son, John Henry felt like he finally had the family he always wanted. He had a nice home, a beautiful wife, a son to spoil and more food than he could ever eat.

Problem was, John Henry's childhood had left him clueless on how to love a woman, let alone be a father and a husband. That and the fact that he worked for one of the biggest drug dealers in California made their relationship troubled at best.

Sheba didn't have great skills in the relationship department either. Her Mother had never been married nor had she had a long-term relationship. Miss Dorothy lived for the con. Running scams and getting money was her claim to fame.

As the years went by, Sheba and John Henry's marital problems increased. They were arguing about silly things like who would pick up Diondre from daycare. The big problem was John Henry's absence. He came home once every few days. And when he was home he found it hard to mentally detach from the violence that was his everyday life. It got to the point where Sheba was practically raising their son alone.

Then the second worst day of John Henry's life happened. Sheba told him she wanted in on the game. She thought getting in the business would help her keep an eye on John Henry. John Henry knew it was a bad idea from the gate. Sheba knew what he did for a living but he'd always kept her far away from the business. Sheba had grown up around scamming, lying and cheating but most of the crimes her mama committed were misdemeanors.

John Henry had argued with her for three days straight trying to change her mind about getting into the business. She was hell bent on doing it and nothing he said—not the horrible things the job brought with it or the fact that she could end up in jail or dead—would make her reconsider.

"Not only am I going to be good at this—I'm gonna be better than you and your bosses. You watch and see. Women know how to run things." She'd told him.

"I'll do this on one condition. You work directly for me."

Sheba nodded her head in agreement. After clearing it with the key people at The Order, John Henry gave her a few of his business accounts. And to his surprise, Sheba was good. *Real* good. A perfect combination of sweet and ruthless, the men respected her and the women bowed down to her.

Sheba rewarded the top performers in her fraction with fabulous parties and expensive gifts. There was gourmet soul food catered by two of the best chefs in town. *Gucci* purses for the women and *Louis Vuitton* wallets for the men. That motivated everyone else to try to outperform the others.

Sheba did so well that some of the other dealers in the cartel got intimidated. John Henry got called into a meeting with the *Big Man*, that's what they called the Supreme Boss. Apparently, one of his high rolling henchman wanted a piece of Sheba's territory—an area she had groomed and developed into a high yielding piece of geography. The Godfather tried to advocate for John Henry but the cartel wasn't having it.

John Henry offered the Big Man one of his own ten block areas—the one that pulled the most money. Big Man turned that money-churning offer down flat. That's when John Henry knew this wasn't about money or seniority—they wanted to take Sheba down a few notches. John Henry knew what his boss was capable of so he cut a deal with him. He also talked his boss into letting him handle Sheba's *relocation*.

He asked to be let out of his contract after he took Sheba down. His boss agreed to let him go after the takeover was complete. John Henry also had to agree to never sling drugs in Socal again.

John Henry set Sheba up to get busted but made sure she had time to shut down shop before the cops got there. Shutting everything down meant she had to wash a half-million in drug money. Everything went according to plan but later, Sheba found out it was John Henry who turned over on her. She didn't believe him when he told her he'd done it to save her life. In the end, the deal cost John Henry the two things he loved more than everything. His wife and his job.

After he retired from slinging in the City of Angels, the Godfather gave John Henry a job doing security for cartel members traveling between the U.S. and Columbia. Like always, after a few years he was promoted to Head of Security. Thankful not to have to do anymore hand to hand combat, he vowed to serve The Godfather until the end. Another change of power took place a few years later. His boss stayed on to serve the leaders of the new organization. They needed somebody to recruit and train security for the big bosses. A few months later, John Henry became the head of strong arm security for The Order.

*****

Sheba's stomach cringed when she saw John Henry's name on the caller ID. She was tempted not to answer. She had enough going on in her life without his drama. She motioned her assistant out of the office. On the third and final ring she broke down and picked up the phone.

"What's up, John Henry?"

"What's this I hear about you putting some green kid on the corner?"

One of her mules had been talking.

"He's a friend of our son. He needed some help. I gave him a lifeline."

"Your *help* has that boy swimming in a pool of sharks and remoras without a lifejacket."

"Stay out of my business and I'll stay out of yours."

He ignored her like he always did. "I'm just saying, what were you thinking, She? This kid is gonna get himself killed or locked up."
"What you gonna tell Diondre when his homeboy becomes a lifer or worse, get deaded, because you made a bad decision?"

"I got this. Is there anything else?"

"How's my boy doing?"

"Why don't you call him and find out?"

"He knows where I live. He can come by here anytime he wants."

"Call your son, John Henry. Take him out to dinner. Ask him what's going on in his life, how he's doing in school, if he has a girlfriend or not."

"You're laying it on kind of thick. He said something to you?"

"All I'm saying is, Dee-dee needs his father. It's not that deep."

"Fine. I'll call him. Anything else Queen Sheba?"

"Yeah, I need a million dollars. You got it?"

"If you were my woman, your paper'd be stacked so high you couldn't even see over the top of it."

She laughed at that. "You're crazy. You know that, right?"

John Henry started laughing too. He was in one of his rare, good moods.

"I gotta run. Don't forget to call your son."

"I said I'll do it. So when we gonna get together? Just for dinner. For old times sake."
"Never."

"Quit tripping, She. We friends aren't we?"

"Stop calling me that."

"Bethsheba Ransome, will you go out to dinner with me?"

She paused before answering, "Maybe. Just to talk about our son."

"Cool. What time you get off work?"

"What makes you think I'm available tonight?"

"I'll send a car by to pick you up around seven. Is that good?"

"Oh, you're balling out of control, huh?"

"See you later. Keep it sweet for me."

"Bye, John Henry."

The only reason she said yes to John Henry's invitation was to find out who in her operation had been telling secrets. At least that's what she told herself....

Twelve

Sheba put a call in to Raymond to let him know she had to work late. His phone went straight to voicemail. That meant he'd run his battery down and had it on the charger waiting for enough juice to turn it back on. That gave her an hour or two before she had to check in.

She called Diondre. She wanted to see if John Henry had kept his word and called his son. She also wanted him to cover for her if dinner with his dad ran late.

"Hey son. I'm gonna be late tonight. Let Raymond know for me?"

"No problem, Mom Dukes. Oh—forgot to tell you. Ray told me to tell you that he's staying at his mom's tonight. She's not feeling so good."

"I'll check on him in a minute. So how was your day?"

"Same old, same. I'm still the Kang."

She chuckled and told him, "Well Mr. Kang, I better get back to work. Tell the Rawmeister to leave me some of that green juice and some vegan spaghetti in the fridge."

"You want some nut cheese on it?"

"Hell yeah."

"Your dad is supposed to call you about taking a vacation this summer. You hear from him?"

"Nope. He's flaking like he always does. Auight moms. Be careful out there. Watch out for the wolves."

"The wolves better watch out for me."

Fifteen minutes to seven, Sheba went to her office closet and took out a simple black dress and a pair of black sandals with straps that snaked around her ankles. She freshened up her hair, rubbed a dab of perfumed oil on her pulse points and headed for the door. John Henry's driver was outside waiting.

A click or two later they pulled up to Patina's, a delightful French Bistro on the outskirts of West Hollywood. She couldn't believe he brought her there. Patina's was their spot when they were an item.

Inside there were candlelit tables, a crackling fire in the dining area, Parisian jazz piping in over the airwaves. John Henry was sitting at the table looking like a royalty. Red shirt, black pants, black Stetson tilted to the side.

She sat down at the table and gave him a dirty look.

John Henry kept the masquerade going. "What's wrong with you?"

"You're playing games, Mr. Henry. You know I'm with Raymond now. Why don't you leave it alone?"

He chuckled and said, "I don't like losing."

"You didn't lose. You gave up."

"Well, I'm tossing my hat back in the ring."

76

"TKO my brother. And so we're clear, that fight is over and done."

She watched the painlight in his eyes come on. Ten seconds later he'd extinguished it. Same way a smoker put out a cigarette.

She rose to leave. "I'm out of here."

"Hold on. Can you at least have a drink with me? Something I want to talk to you about."

She paused, stared at him for a few, finally sat back down. "This better be good."

"I'm buying the house. Wanna make sure you and Dee-dee are taken care of. In case...case something happens to me, the house is also in your name."

"What're you talking about? Dee-Dee already has a house. And nothing's gonna happen to you. You're like Popeye. You eat your can of spinach and snap back like new."

"There's only one problem. *You* were my can of spinach."

"I gotta go, John Henry. Talk to you later."

"It's like that?"

"It's *so* like that."

"Can a brother get a hug?"

She ventured into the danger zone to hug him.

He drew her close to him. She felt his solid body against hers. The kitty kat gave her a warning meow. She backed up like she'd put her hand on a hot stove.

"I'm outta here. Deuces."

She looked back at him as she moved through the door. His faced was flushed. She knew blood was rushing to his lower parts turning him into the savage she loved to bone.

The ride home she thought about John Henry buying their old house. When they were together she'd begged him to get out of the game and settle down with her. He turned her down cold. Said permanent residences were for suckers who believed in the American dream. Told her he was a gangsta and gangsters were rolling stones. That was the day she decided to bury that stone called John Henry Carter and never look back.

Her emergency cell phone buzzed with a Jay Z ringtone and killed the painful memories swimming in her head. When her red cell phone rang, it meant trouble, big trouble. Wisdom's voice—Wisdom was one of her main Queenpins-- shook like a five pointer as she told her what had gone down on one of their corners....

"My source told me that The Godfather did a drive by to check out one of our mules. Fabian didn't know who he was and started flapping his gums. He was bragging about how large we are and how this is just the beginning. Told him we're gonna take over the whole city."

Sheba's stomach did a back flip. "Pull his stupid ass off the streets and put him on a desk until further notice."

"Wish I could boss lady but nobody can find him. My source say he's riding around in The Godfather's stretch limo toking chronic and sipping yack."

"Shit. The Godfather's probably pumping him for info. I'm gonna have to call in a favor to get him out of there. Good looking out, Wisdom. You go on back to work. I'll text you an update when I have one."

The France-born-America-living Kingpin they called *The Godfather* was a legend in West Los Angeles. Word had it that he was the bankroll behind the 90's film classic, *White Boys Can't Jump*. He'd earned street cred for branding the marijuana blend affectionately known by its users as the *Chronic*. The Godfather's temper was fire and ice. He'd pump six rounds into a disobedient salesman and two minutes later be chilling on the beach like a hippy. He was known for his love of the Beegee's classics hits which he liked to listen to while puffing on a fat J.

The Godfather made so much money slinging pot, that in the early 2000's, he upgraded to cocaine. Now The Godfather's street team was responsible for moving at least half of the Girl in SoCal's sand and surf communities. The only territory he didn't have on his payroll was a twenty-block stretch in West Los Angeles that everybody in their business called, *Ransome Blvd.*

Sheba had known The Godfather since she was a child. Her Mother had helped him get his operation started. The

Godfather and Sheba's Mother pulled strings for each other whenever the situation called for it. Then John Henry started working for him full time.

She had no connection to him other than his being her husband's boss. But even after her Mother passed away, The Godfather had kept in touch with her. Every Christmas and on her birthday he sent Sheba exquisite gifts. She didn't know why he did it but she knew better than to reject his kindness.

Sheba didn't want to let John Henry know he was right about her making a bad decision in hiring Fabian so she reached out to The Godfather's assistant. A tall drink of water named Amber with boobs and butt that'd cost at least twenty grand. Amber directed her to a watering hole on Lincoln Blvd in the Marina where The Godfather went to drink and play with bikini dancers. Sheba called the bar and asked to speak to him.

The password to speak with The Godfather hadn't changed in a decade. When the phone girl asked for the secret code, Sheba spat it out like it was bad food.

"White girl."

Two minutes later his smooth voice greeted her like they were old friends.

"Shebahhhh. To what do I owe the pleasure of hearing your lovely voice?"

The Godfather loved his social niceties. She played along with it, treated him like he was a Hollywood mogul.

"Bonjour. Comment allez-vous?"

"J'ai faim. Ca vous dit d'aller manger?

She answered him in English. "I would love to get a bite to eat. In fact, why don't you let my chef prepare something fabulous for us?

"Ahhh—food is my medicine. What's his specialty?"

"Choucroute garnie. He imports the sausages from Paris. Makes the sauce from scratch. It's delectable."

"Ahhhh, a meal from my homeland. Sounds delightful. I'll be there around nine?"

"Perfect! Uh…can you bring my employee with you? I need to talk with him about his little fantasies."

The Godfather chuckled and said, "He did mention your interest in selling your wares at several of my establishments."

The Godfather was fishing, trying to see if there was meat to go with Fabian's make-believe potatoes.

"He was really trying to impress you. He's a childhood friend of my son. Tried to give him a shot at a real job but I don't think he has the right skills."

"He *is* a little green."

Same thing John Henry said.

"Just so you know, we're perfectly happy where we are. We've got so much work we're bordering on being overwhelmed. And you know I wouldn't make a move without your blessings."

"After all these years, I thought you understood how things went. But everybody needs a little reminder every now and then."

"Just a dumb kid."

She could hear him thinking, contemplating whether she was telling the truth.

"I'll take you up on that dinner. We'll dine in honor of your mother, the wolf of all wolves. And I'll have my driver drop off your iceberg lettuce. You have a good evening, Bethsheba Ransome."

"Merci."

His tone let her know that he was satisfied. That meant he wouldn't wage a war on her thriving business.

She called ahead to the Rawmeister so he could get dinner going. Raymond and Diondre were out doing their thing so there was nothing to worry about there. Maybe this would turn out well. She and The Godfather could deepen their business connection and he would give her more real estate to expand her territory.

Sheba thought she was out of the woods until she stuck the key in the door of Ransome Castle and discovered an unexpected guest.

Thirteen

Rebecca Harmon.   Her son Diondre's college crush. The only girl he'd ever brought home for Sheba to give the once over.

She looked like a thicker, more sophisticated version of the singer, *Rhianna*. Short pixie cut with hot pink highlights, British designer clothes, six-hundred-dollar boots that she'd be tired of in two weeks and an ass that worked overtime.

Rebecca was parked on a plush couch in the family room, legs tucked, watching VH1 and chomping on buttery popcorn.

"Hi, Mama Sheba. Diondre told me to wait for him here. He gave me the key.

"Dee should've checked with me. What time is he getting in here?"

"Around ten."

Sheba thought fast. "I'm gonna have my driver drop you off at home. I have a private meeting with someone very important and..."

"Can I just stay here? Promise I'll be quiet. Told Dee-dee I'd be here when he got home and well...he doesn't like it when I break my word."

"It's not going to work. I have a very important meeting and there can be no interruptions."

"I won't make a sound."

Sheba had a short window to change clothes and brainstorm her strategy to get The Godfather batting for her side of the team again.

"I need you to stay out of the way. I mean it. Unless the house is burning down or you need a kidney—don't interrupt my meeting. Understood?"

"Yes, Mama Ransome."

Sheba really liked Rebecca. From her POV, all the other girls Dee-dee had dated were golddiggers—chippees looking for a man to finance their hair weaves and designer clothes. Not Rebecca. Becca was smart, a high achiever—definitely a top shelf breeder.

Only problem was Rebecca was a lamb. Sheba worried she wouldn't be strong enough to handle Dee-dee when he was in warrior mode. Diondre was the son of a gangster father and a wolf mother.

She'd raised him to have manners. Taught him how to treat a lady. But there was another side of his gene pool—John Henry's side. Bottom line was, the woman Dee-dee married had to have a steel fist inside of her white glove.

The doorbell chimed announcing Sheba's guest had arrived. She clicked on the doorcam and saw The Godfather and his henchmen standing on her porch. She pressed the intercom and let him know someone would be right down to fetch him.

Sheba wore a floor length black dress with a slit up the thigh for her soiree with The Godfather. Around her neck was a thin gold chain holding a solitaire diamond. Her hair was swept up in a neat chignon with a rhinestone hairpin in the center. She knew image was everything to The Godfather and had gone the extra mile to ensure her appearance was flawless.

The Rawmeister took The Godfather's jacket and offered him a glass of champagne. As usual The Godfather was dressed impeccably. Black *Brooks Brothers* suit with a crisp white shirt. White brim with a black band. A large diamond stud in his right ear was the only bling he wore. He looked like an older version of The Rock.

"Sheeeeebahhhh. You look stunning. Your mother would be proud."

He kissed the backside of her hand, inhaled her sweet perfume into his nostrils like it was a drug.

Sheba put on the sugar, "You know you were her favorite. Mama always talked about how much she loved cooking for you."

"Your mother's swine was the only pork I'd eat. There will always be a soft spot beneath this alligator skin for Empress Ransome."

"Relax. Have a seat. May I get your guests anything?"

The Godfather waved his guys away. "They're just here to watch over an old man. Make sure I don't trip and fall on anything. I can have them wait outside if you prefer."

Sheba nodded and chuckled knowingly. The Godfather's *guests* were highly trained marksmen. Mercenaries who killed without blinking or thinking. They took his subtle cue and headed for the door.

The Rawmeister made an announcement.

"Dinner is served, Madam. Sir."

She turned to The Godfather. "Join me in the dining room."

The Godfather took her hand like they were at a ball.

"After you, Miss Ransome. Or is it Missus?"

"Still Miss."

"I was just telling John Henry that he was a fool to let you swim away. But you know what they say—one man's ex is another man's treasure."

She motioned at the seat. "Very true indeed. Sit. Eat. Enjoy this fabulous meal prepared in your honor!"

After five courses of the Rawmeister's delicious cooking and a few glasses of top shelf bubbly, The Godfather was primed for some real talk.

First she dismissed the Rawmeister. The Godfather had a known rule about not discussing business around anyone except his chosen constituents. Sheba had to make sure he knew they were alone and could talk business.

"If you'll excuse me for just a minute, I'm going to release my housestaff for the evening."

The Godfather nodded his understanding.

A few minutes later Sheba returned to the table. She approached him carefully. She knew the wrong words could make him back peddle with a quickness.

"Did my lettuce make it home alright?"

"Yeah…we dropped him off at his place of residence. Your mule admitted he was writing fairytales. We're good now. *Ransome 2K* is back on track."

"That's good to hear. You're like an uncle to me. I cherish the understanding we've had over the years."

Sheba noticed that The Godfather kept staring at her. It was like he was looking for something. It kind of creeped her out.

He fiddled with his napkin as he told her, "I made your mother a promise before she died. Told her I would watch over you."

Sheba hadn't known about the promise. Made her sad to think about Mama. She choked back her emotions and summoned her wolf demeanor to continue sizing up the prey.

"Mama always had something up her sleeve didn't she?"

"She did indeed. There is something else I want to talk to you about. I have some property on the Westside that my guys can't seem to move. Need a special team to move this real estate."

She popped an olive in her mouth and gave him a cool answer. "I'd be glad to take a look at it for you."

The Godfather went on about how his unmanned spot on the Westside was a prime area. Had the potential to move twenty to fifty to a hundred G a day.

"Manhattan Beach is filled with beach houses and Benzes, rich doctors and crooked lawyers who love their medicinal. We can be their supplier."

If Ransome got that territory….

Sheba was about to move in for the kill when a small voice snatched her from her revelry. Sheba almost went into shock.

"Mama Ransome, I'm really sorry to bother you. I know you're in an important meeting but the cable went out and Nick Cannon was just about to announce the winner. *"*

When The Godfather snapped his head toward Rebecca's voice, Sheba's heart dropped into her stomach. The Godfather picked up his cell and called in the dogpound. In minutes, The Godfather's henchmen were standing next to him, legs spread, right hand inside the left side of their coats where the guns were.

Kingpins didn't take kindly to unannounced, uncleared guests at their private meetings. Rebecca had stepped into a circle of danger. Once again, one of Dee-dee's little friends was interfering with her business.

Sheba went into damage control.

Through a grimacing smile Sheba said, "Becca, honey, Mother-in-law told you I couldn't be disturbed."

Rebecca looked confused for a minute then caught on.

"I'm sorry, Mama Sheba! Thought your company had already gone."

"Excuse my manners. This is Rebecca Harmon, my soon to be daughter-in-law."

The Godfather's face seemed to relax a little. He leaned back on the couch and picked up his champagne.
"What's your name again pretty one?"

"Rebecca Evelene Harmon. Nice to meet you Mister…"

"Peters. Robert Peters." The Godfather said smiling like death.

"I've seen you somewhere….you're a cheerleader?"

"Yes! For the Bruins football team!"

Sheba knew The Godfather was collecting all the information he needed in case any intel from their meeting was leaked.

Rebecca turned to leave. Her tight body and bubble booty danced a sensual number before she spun around to leave them.

"Forgive my manners. Have a good evening, Mr. Peters."

"You too Rebecca."

The Godfather sat in silence for a few minutes.

"Can you ask your butler to bring my jacket?"

"He's gone for the evening. I'll get it for you. Are you rushing off? Thought we could finish our conversation."

"You've got company. It would be rude."

"They're getting married in a few months. She came by to talk about the wedding. We're good."

Sheba knew he wasn't going for it. The Godfather had trust issues. And in his line of work, he should. He only talked business in the presence of his tried and tested.

"Another time. Another place."

"I'm very interested in your proposition."

"Another time, another place, Sheba Ransome."

The Godfather hated to repeat himself. People who did business with him knew that was one of his pet peeves. When he repeated himself that meant he was one notch from an outburst. An outburst with The Godfather could mean you lost a finger or worse, death.

Sheba had to cool him off before he left.

"You can't leave without having dessert. The Rawmeister made homemade French Vanilla Ice Cream and baked Tiramisu."

The Godfather licked his lips, rubbed his potbelly and eased back down into the chair. Sheba knew food was one of his weaknesses. Sheba rushed to the kitchen and retrieved a large silver tray bearing two saucers of the delectable dessert and homemade vanilla ice cream. She sat the tray down and stretched a white linen napkin across The Godfather's lap. She placed the dessert before him like it was a plate of diamonds then poured a cup of steaming hot coffee into one of the two Herringbone china cups.

The sweet smells rising from the table were almost an aphrodisiac. The Godfather let out a long moan as the sweet gooey chocolate and cool vanilla crème joined forces on his tongue.

"This is nirvana," he said as his spirit went back to a nice place.

"Does it make you feel good?" Sheba asked, using her feminine wiles to calm the beast in him.

Before he answered, The Godfather scrolled through what seemed to be a very important text message. Sheba knew The Godfather's tech team had just run a background check on Rebecca. He seemed relieved by whatever the results were but he had a few more questions about Sheba's son's girlfriend before he continued their meeting.

"Very good. But I think I know what would make everything right. We could close this business deal tonight."

"Anything. Just name it."

He said her name like she was an item on a menu.

"Rebecca Evelene Harmon."

Sheba swallowed hard, tried to calm her already rattled nerves.

"My son's little chippie? You don't want her. I mean, we can do so much better than that."

As soon as the words came out of her mouth, Sheba knew she had chosen the wrong strategy. People always wanted the untouchable. What a person couldn't have was always more attractive than what they could easily obtain.

She tried to clean it up. "But if that's what you've set your sights on, it's no big deal."

The Godfather's mouth spread into a wicked smile. "I want *her*. Before I leave tonight."

Sheba was sure she'd just had a coronary. In fact, she almost wished she did. An ambulance and two big burly paramedics bursting through the door would kill this nightmare that was getting worse by the minute.

"I'll talk to her but if you think Fabian was green—this one here is yellow. She's an innocent. No experience whatsoever. I can get you somebody with a grown woman's skills and young girl's body. Give me a few minutes and I'll make some calls to..."

The Godfather nodded. "Go on back there and have a little talk. While I wait, can you get me a little more of this dessert your chef made? It's delicious. And a spot of tea would be grand."

Sheba served The Godfather a second helping of Tiramisu and brought him a cup of tea before taking one of the longest walks of her life.

Fourteen

Sheba wished she could hit the rewind button and start the whole night over again.
She was about to commit an act of betrayal so great that if it ever came out—she could lose the one person she cared about more than anyone in the world.

Rebecca was Diondre's first love--the girl he promised to marry when the time was right. She had been a virgin when they met. Dee-dee's organ was the only flesh that'd ever touched her vagina. Becca was the kind of girl who volunteered for *Habitat for Humanity* on the weekends. She didn't even smoke an occasional joint like regular people.

If Sheba refused—if she turned down The Godfather's request—she would forfeit a deal that could position her to knock John Henry off his throne for good. She would get it all back, everything she'd lost. But at what cost?

Maybe this—Rebecca's weakness—needed to be exposed. If she gave in and slept with The Godfather, that was proof she couldn't be trusted. And if she couldn't be trusted, they needed to know now, not later when Dee-dee was raking in the millions.

With all that could be lost or gained, Sheba prayed still that Becca had snuck out of the back door. She fantasized that her son's girlfriend had broken out in hives and had to be rushed to the hospital. But when she opened the door to the family room, Rebecca was there sitting on the sofa, watching VH1 and munching on popcorn.

"TV's working now. I had accidentally pressed the power button on the cable box."

"That's good, Rebecca. I need to talk with you about something. It's very important."

"Sure, Mama Sheba. Want me to cut the TV off?"

"That would be best."

Sheba sat down next to her, took a deep breath and transformed into the wolf she was.

"You remember I told you I had a really important meeting tonight?"

Rebecca nodded and swallowed some iced tea to wash down her corn.

"That man in there is a notorious drug dealer. He's here because one of Dee-Dee's friends got caught slinging in his territory. The Kingpin, he…he knew my mother. He came by to talk to me about it. He's going to kill Dee-dee's friend if we don't do something."

"Oh my God! What can we do to help him? Does he want money? I can call my parents and…"

"No, he has lots of money. What he wants is something he doesn't have."

"I'll do anything to help Dee-dee's friend."

"I'm really glad to hear you say that. One day, you're going to be Dee-Dee's wife and I need to know that if he was in danger, you could keep him safe. Tonight, I'm gonna test you. I need you to put on your big girl panties and do something for me."

"Sure Mama Ransome. Anything."

"I need you to close your eyes, open your legs and let the Kingpin hit it real quick. He's old and it won't take long. I…"

"You're kidding right?"

"It's either that or he's going to kill Dee-dee's best friend. Under these circumstances, I know Dee-dee would understand."

"I want to help but I can't do that Mama Sheba. I just can't."

"Fine. When we're at the funeral, you be sure to tell Dee-dee why his friend is laying their dead."

Rebecca started crying.

"I…I don't even know him."

She was choking and gagging.

"OMG, I think I'm gonna throw up."

"Calm down, Becca. This really isn't a big deal. Five minutes and it'll be over. I'll take you shopping for a new

Gucci backpack and you'll forget it ever happened. You'll be saving Dee-dee's best friend's life."

Tearfully, Rebecca said, "He has to wear a condom."

Sheba smiled. "Of course he does. Now you go in my room and get undressed. I'll send him in in about five minutes. Wipe your eyes and remember what I told you. Pretend you like it and it'll go a lot faster."

Rebecca stood up and headed toward Sheba's bedroom. She stopped at the door.
"Mama Ransome. Promise me you won't tell Dee-dee about this."

"You have my word."

Sheba walked at a snail's pace back to the living room. The Godfather's henchmen had come back inside. The Godfather looked up at her and waited for an answer.

"She's ready for you. Make sure you use a condom."

The Godfather rose from the couch. Sheba took his hand and led him to her bedroom. His henchmen followed closely.

When they got to her bedroom door Sheba stopped him.

"Three things. One—I take over the Manhattan Beach region with a 70% cut. Two—my security guys are on your police officer's payroll. And three, you're extra gentle with Rebecca."

The Godfather stuck out his hand. "Deal."

"And I'm gonna need your Mercs to wait outside by the car until you're finished."

"No problem." He turned to his henchmen. "Go get some food for you and the men. If I'm not out in two hours, come get me." The Godfather commanded.

The Godfather walked down the hall like he lived there, like he was used to sleeping with strange women in other people's homes.

Sheba opened her bedroom door. Saw Rebecca's clothes folded neatly on the chair. Rebecca was in the bed with the covers tucked under her naked chin. She looked so young and innocent laying in the center of her and Raymond's humongous bed.

Without a word, Sheba left him there. Her feet felt as heavy as lead as she trotted down the hall to wait for him to finish doing his business.

Ten nail-biting minutes had gone by when Sheba's bladder forced her to visit the lavatory. She dashed down the hall to the guest bathroom. The moment she flushed she heard someone call her name. She yanked her panties up, rolled her dress down and darted out into the hall.

In the hallway, Diondre was standing at her bedroom door knocking and yelling. "Mama, guess what! We won! We won the championship. Mama, can I come in?"

Fifteen

In her mind, she'd stopped him from walking into the horrific scene going down in her bedroom. In real time her feet were stuck, frozen by the fear of her baby boy knowing what his Mother had let happen. By the time she snapped back to the real world it was too late. Diondre was already in the room.

When Diondre saw The Godfather sitting on the edge of his Mother's bed and his girlfriend naked under the covers he lost it.

"What the fuck!? Becca, what…what's going on?"

Shocked and ashamed, Rebecca sat up abruptly. The sheet fell down exposing her small plump breasts. She snatched the sheet up and wrapped it around her body. She was speechless, incapable of explaining the how or the why to the man she loved.

Dee-dee trained his eyes on The Godfather. "What are you doing in my mama's bed with my girlfriend?"

The Godfather told him, "This isn't personal, son. Don't make it that way. This is business."

Rebecca pleaded with him, "Dee-dee, you don't understand. Nothing happened. I agreed to do it so that…."

Sheba cut in before things got out of hand.

"Becca, go put your clothes on. Go on home and let Dee-dee call you a little later. Mama Ransome needs to clear a few things up with Diondre and my friend."

Rebecca started crying hysterically. "He doesn't understand. I did it because...."

"Don't worry. Everything's gonna be okay. It's all a big misunderstanding."

Sheba winked at The Godfather. Her eyes begged him not to tell her son what went down.

Diondre had rage oozing from his pores. He was staring The Godfather down. His expression was downright disgust and hate.

"Motherfucker, I oughta beat you down."

"Sheba, you better get your son. He's starting to piss me off."

Dee-dee ran over to the closet, reached into a purple shoebox with yellow writing and took out her 357 Mag. He walked back over to the bed and pointed the gun at The Godfather's head.

"Nobody touches what's mine."

For the first time ever, Sheba saw fear in The Godfather's eyes.

The Godfather told him. "Calm down little Dee-dee. Let me talk to you."

"I think he was gonna rape her, Mama. This fat ass pimp was getting ready to violate my woman."

Without flinching The Godfather said, "The Godfather doesn't need to take pussy from any woman."

Diondre cocked the gun and said, "What you say, man?"

"Look, boy. You're making a mistake. You need to talk to your Mother."

"Dee-dee, give me the gun. Give me that gun right now!" Sheba yelled at him.

"She'd never lay down with garbage like you."

The Godfather had had enough. "Your mother told her...."

Horrified that The Godfather was about to tell Diondre what she did, Sheba went to grab the gun. He held on for dear life as Sheba tried to wrench it from his hands.

Their struggle was interrupted when Sheba heard a loud thud. Her heart stopped. Time froze. She heard something heavy drop. It nicked her foot before it hit the floor. She looked down and saw her gun lying at her feet. She shoved her son away from her and searched for blood on his clothes and then hers. Dee-dee's clothes were clean as a whistle. Her body was free of bullet holes. She whipped her head around in The Godfather's direction.

"No, Dee-dee, no! What have you gone and done?"

Sixteen

With his mouth in the shape of a perfect O, The Godfather looked at them in disbelief. Then he leaned to the right and fell sideways like a bowling pin onto the floor.

"Call...call an ambulance." He demanded as death stepped into the room and introduced itself.

Sheba gasped as blood poured from a wound just beneath The Godfather's left shoulder.

Dee-dee went into shock. "Mama, mama, maaaa-maaaaaa."

"Diondre, call 911!" Sheba yelled.

Diondre stood there staring, tears pooling in the corner of his eyes as The Godfather faded like a rose at the end of summer.

"I di-di-didn't mean to shoo—shoot him."

The Godfather's eyes were rolling back in his head.

"Too late for that now. Call 911!" Sheba screamed.

The Godfather gasped, stretched his arm out to them and took a short flight to that place people go after their heart stops pumping.

Sheba knew they had to think fast or she and Diondre would be joining The Godfather at his final destination.

She grabbed her phone and did what she always did when the bottom fell out of her life. She called John Henry.

He answered before her Nicki Minaj ring tone finished the first verse.

"What's up, She?"

"Dee-dee....your son just shot somebody."

"What? Who my boy pop a cap on?"

"He....The Godfather. Him and The Godfather got into it because..."
"What the fuck you talking about? This some kind of joke?"

"Look, this isn't a joke and I need you to get your ass over here. Now!"

"I'll be there in fifteen."

Fifteen minutes later John Henry was strolling through the room where she and Raymond made love, shared secrets and pain. He'd come in through the service entrance so The Godfather's henchmen wouldn't see him.

Diondre was sitting on the floor with his back against the wall. His tear-stained face was still frozen in fear. When his eyes connected with his Dad's, Diondre asked, "I'm going to prison ain't I dad?

John Henry glanced toward the bed, saw The Godfather stretched out like he was ready to be carried out feet first.

"Ain't nobody going to jail, son. Sheba, how in the hell you let something like this happen?"

"It...it's complicated."

Before she could explain further, The Godfather's phone starting buzzing. Sheba knew it was probably his mercs calling, checking in on their meal ticket.

Sheba paced back and forth. "We gotta do something fast."

"Is he dead?"

"I'm not sure."

John Henry felt The Godfather's neck for a pulse. "I think he's still alive. You gotta tell me what went down."

She looked over at her son. "Dee-dee, go down the hall and wash your face. Your dad and I need to talk. Hurry up, son. We don't have a lot of time."

Dazed and traumatized by what just went down, Diondre stood on wobbly legs.

"I'm sorry, Ma. I shouldn't have...."

"We'll talk later, son."

After he was gone, John Henry picked up the murder weapon and started cleaning it.

"Talk."

"The Godfather picked up one of my mules. Fabian. He had been running his chops about how we were gonna take over territory."

"I told you not to put him out there. Told you the nigga was green. You never listen to me. Why She? What the hell were you thinking?"

"This is the not the time to lecture me, John Henry. Anyway, The Godfather was gonna make him go *pop goes the weasel*. I intervened—reminded him how much my mama did to help his operation. He agreed to let the boy off the hook if my chef hooked up a gourmet meal in his honor. During dinner he offered me a sweet deal to take over one of his prime territories. Then Dee-dee's little girlfriend interrupted us and the bottom fell out of my dream. The girl wasn't supposed to be here! Dee-dee gave her the house key without my permission. I didn't have time to get her out. So I asked her to stay out of dodge."

"You should've put her ass out on the street when you walked in the door. You're getting soft in your old age. The Sheba I knew had way more game than that."

"Dee-dee's little chippy disobeyed. That was the domino that made all the others fall."

"What did The Godfather do to her?"

"He wanted her forbidden fruit. Told me he'd overlook the fact that I had a stranger in the house while we were talking business if I let him hit it. What could I say? Everybody knows The Godfather doesn't talk business in the presence of strangers. I couldn't let him think my game was weak so I tried to convince him she was safe. He called my bluff."

"Something ain't adding up. The Godfather's stable is filled with the most beautiful women in the city. Sleeping with Dee-dee's girl is breaking the code."

Sheba wondered how John Henry knew so much about The Godfather's operation. Then she remembered he'd worked for him for a short stint back in the day.

"Maybe he did it to prove a point. People always want what they think is unattainable."

"So you pimped out your son's girlfriend so you could get in good with The Godfather."

"It wasn't like that! She wasn't supposed to be here."

"Well, she *was* here."

Before they could finish their convo, The Godfather groaned the groan of a dying man. Their heads snapped around to where he was laying.

"Oh. My. God. He's waking up!"

Seventeen

"Help....help me. I can't breathe."

Sheba couldn't believe those words were coming from the man thousands feared and loathed simultaneously.

She thought about helping him—she even stood up to call 911. Then her wolf kicked in and activated one of the laws that ruled her Queedom:

Preserve the pack at all costs.

"We gotta finish him, John Henry. If we leave him alive we're dead for sure."

"You're crazy. Kill him and the whole damn Order will be at your door by the morning."

Sheba snatched The Godfather's phone off the bed.

"We need time." She said it out loud but was talking to herself.

"What are you doing, She?"

"I need the code to his cell." She punched random numbers into his cell.

"For what?"

She used her index finger to poke The Godfather a few inches from his bullet wound. He grimaced in pain.

"Tell me the code and I'll call you an ambulance."

"My guys will be here in a few minutes. You better run now if you want see daylight again."

Sheba grabbed the gun off the floor, poked it into the spot where he'd been wounded. "Give me the code now or the game's over!"

"779311." The Godfather whimpered with the little strength he had left.

Sheba entered the code.

"I'm in. What name are your Mercs under?"

"Coyote."

She sent The Godfather's henchmen a text telling them that it would be another hour.

"I just bought us an hour."

John Henry paced the floor. He always paced when he was in trouble.

"I hope you know what you're doing."

"There's only one way out of this. We have to kill him, get rid of the body and blow town."

"That's not gonna work. I need you to calm down so we can think this through."

Sheba was scrolling through his phone reading text messages.

"We can't leave him alive. He's not the kind of enemy you can live with."

"The Godfather isn't the kind of man you can just kill and forget about. Sheba?"

"Yeah, I heard you." She was deep into the content on The Godfather's cell phone.

Suddenly Sheba's eyes bulged out of their sockets like she'd just seen a snake.

"You gotta be shitting me. You're not going to believe what I just found in his phone. It's all here. Merc orders, kill photos, bank accounts, names of everybody in his operation. I got him, John Henry."

"Who keeps that kind of intel on their phone?"

"Somebody who doesn't trust computers."

John Henry took the phone from her and skimmed a few folders. Saw enough intel to crucify The Godfather and several key figures in his operation.

"She, there's something you need to know about The Godfather."

"It doesn't matter. With this kind of intel I can squash him like an ant. We're shutting this mofo down."

"This—what I'm talking about—it matters."

Sheba wasn't really listening. She was heading to her office to plug The Godfather's phone into her computer. John Henry followed her.

"Sheba, you need to listen to me."

She half-listened while she copied The Godfather's files and records onto a flash drive.

"The names of every Don from here to Puerto Rico are here along with their financial holdings. Instead of killing him, I think I'm gonna blackmail him. Force him to retire. If any harm comes to me or our family, his info will be sent to every media network in the globe."

"Sheba, if you don't hurry up and get him to a hospital, he's gonna dead out on you. After that, every merc in Cali will have your pic in their phone."

"Why would they come after me? I'll say he left out of the back entrance. They can't prove anything."

"I'm trying to tell you something about this situation that you don't know. Something you really need to know. Something I should've told you long time ago. Something your Mother told me."

Sheba's fingers froze in place.

She turned to John Henry. "What does my mother have to do with this? What could my mother have told you that she didn't tell me?"

"I need you to calm down and listen, Sheba." He knew how sensitive she was about her Mother.

"I know she covered for him when he killed some man. They were about to send his ass up the river for three decades but Mama lied for him. Said he was with her when everything went down."

"That's not all."
"What is it, John Henry? I have thirty-five minutes left before his goons bust through my front door. Stop bullshitting and tell me what's going on!"

"The Godfather is your people. He's your father, She."

"What the fuck are you talking about? My Daddy is dead. He disappeared two months after I was born. Mama said he was murdered."

"She lied to you. Your Moms didn't want you getting caught up in that life. She swore The Godfather to secrecy in exchange for her testifying for him."

"Secrecy about what?"

"The truth about what happened the night of the murder. And that he's your father. Why do you think he used to come see on your birthdays."

"I thought….thought he was indebted to Mama for her not ratting him out."

"No She, he was coming to see *you*. His daughter."

"So you're saying the man lying in there dying on my bed is my father? And our son Diondre....Diondre just shot his grandfather?"

"That's what I'm saying."

"I don't believe you, John Henry."

Sheba stormed back down the hall to her bedroom and flung the door open. The Godfather had slithered across the floor a few inches but was unable to stand up.

Sheba grabbed him by the lapels of his three thousand-dollar blazer, pulled his face up to hers and glared into his bloodshot eyes. She thought about all the people he had killed, all the pregnant mothers hooked on his powder and dope.

She seethed with disgust at the thought that a pure demon seed, a downright devil spawn like The Godfather could be her father.

"One question. Tell me the truth and I'll let you go. Are you my father?"

In response to her question, The Godfather did something she'd never seen him do. He cried.

Not when her mother died, not even when he was close to taking his last breath had he shed a tear. But when she asked him that question, his eyes welled up with tears. He swallowed hard before answering her.

"Yes, Sheba. I....I'm your father."

"Noooooooooooo!!!!! This is not happening!" She banged him on the chest before she let him go.

After coughing up a few tablespoons of blood he told her, "I…I wanted to tell you but your Mother said…your Mother said she would have me locked up. She had me…had me on tape admitting I murdered a man."

"And you were going to sleep with my son's girlfriend— your granddaughter???"

"I wasn't gonna have sex with that girl. I wanted…wanted to test her for Diondre. See if she could be trusted. I never…I never touched her. You can ask her."

"Why didn't you tell me after Mama died? Why!!!!"

The Godfather passed out before he could answer. Sheba thought he had died.

"Call 911!"

"What are you going to say?"

"I'll tell them he accidently shot himself."

"Is your gun registered?"

"Yes, the ones at home are clean."

As John Henry punched in the numbers, The Godfather mumbled something through his teeth.

John Henry walked over to him. "What? What are you saying? Speak up, man!"

"Don't....don't call 911. Dial 469...on my phone. It's a private doctor and... ambulance service. They'll take care of me." His voice trailed off into lala land again.

"What about your henchmen? What do I tell them when they come back?"

"They'll get the intel about me on a special network. Make that call. I don't have long."

Sheba dialed the number on his phone. Twenty minutes later, an ambulance pulled into the driveway through the service entrance.

The paramedics loaded The Godfather on the ambulance bed, heaved the gurney up and into the van. Diondre came over to where they were standing and posted up next to John Henry. Sheba wondered where he'd been when they were talking.

John Henry asked, "You going with him, She?"

She nodded her head. "Take care of Dee-dee. Tell Raymond I'm at the hospital with a friend. I'll explain what happened later."

As the ambulance spun off, Sheba peered through the window at Diondre who was standing on the sundeck next to John Henry. She wondered if he knew his Mother had traded his girl to come up in the drug business.

She wondered if he knew she'd put his best friend in the game knowing it would swallow him up and spit out his bones. And the worst part of all, did he hear that a heartless savage named The Godfather was his mother's father and his grandfather?

What Sheba wished he knew—what she didn't have a chance to tell him—was that she'd done it all for him. She did it so that in five years they wouldn't have to worry about money ever again. She'd done it because running game was in her blood and being a wolf was all she knew. The question was, could and would he ever forgive her?

Eighteen

When they got to the hospital they rushed The Godfather into surgery. The bullet had lodged an inch from his left lung. It was a miracle they were able to stop the bleeding. After they got the bullet out, they worked to stabilize him. The doctors at this unit were used to working on gunshot victims. Their main clientele was crooks and criminals.

The Order had already been contacted by the ambulance drivers. The Godfather's superiors were in route to the hospital. The Coyotes—the Godfather's mercs—drove in behind them but fell back as they pulled into the ER. In the hospital, two huge security guards escorted Sheba to a small room with a couch and coffeepot. When they left, they took her cell phone and locked the door. What they didn't know was the phone they took was a dummy phone. Her real phone was in a pouch at the small of her back.

Sheba knew Raymond was going crazy because he couldn't reach her. All hell was going to break loose if he didn't hear from her real soon.

As soon as The Godfather woke up he asked for Sheba. He knew if the mob got to her first, it was over. They had to get their stories in sync and he had to make sure Sheba didn't say anything about the information she'd gotten off his phone. Daughter or not, they kill her in a heartbeat to protect the Order.

Sheba followed the guards down the hall to The Godfather's room. A myriad of questions raced through her mind as she approached the door.

The Godfather's raspy voice snatched her out of the dark thoughts she was draped in. It felt like she was in a dream or more like a nightmare. She wished it *was* a dream and she could wake up wrapped in Raymond's sweet smell and the safety of his embrace.

She looked down at her father. "So...you made it through."

"Yeah, it's kind of hard to kill a pit bull."

As if he were reading her mind, before she could ask, he said, "I guess you have some questions for me."

"Yeah, I do have a few."

"Shoot. Just not at me this time." He chuckled lightly.

"First question. Why didn't you marry her?"

"It's a long story. But the short of it is because I wasn't the marrying kind. Being the wife of a drug dealer is no life for a woman or a mother. The kind of people I hang around— you and Dorothy were safer if nobody knew we were related."
She thought about how hard it had been in her marriage to John Henry. The long hours. All the time away from home. The nights he came home covered in blood. The smell of women's perfume on his clothes.

"How do you know John Henry?"

"He worked for me when he was a kid."

John Henry had told the truth about that. She had a feeling there was more to the story but today wasn't the day for that conversation.

The Godfather tried to move and flinched in pain. He was still pretty groggy from the medication. He sucked it up and told her what she needed to know to stay alive.

"There's something else you should know."

"I'm listening."

"The man I killed when you were eight years old—you know why I did what I did right?"

"That was question number three."

"I killed him because he was being inappropriate with you."

"What do you mean by inappropriate?"

"You know what I mean."

"Are you saying he was trying to molest me? Did my mother know about that?"

"Yes, that's what I'm saying. And yes, she knew. But this man was important to her operation. She wanted to handle it her own way. I wasn't having it."

Sheba didn't understand. Why would her Mother protect a man who was trying to molest her? The Godfather tried to explain.

"She was angry with me. She had been looking for a way to get back at me because I didn't marry her when she got pregnant with you."

"I know my Mother was...special. They didn't call her a wolf for nothing."

"Think I don't know? I created that monster. But she gave me you so that made up for everything."

Sheba choked back the tears, called her inner wolf forward and attended to the business at hand. "What do you want to do about...about what happened?"

The Godfather knew that the room might be wired so he chose his words carefully. "It was an accident. You were showing me a gun. You didn't know it was loaded. It went off. End of story."

"What am I supposed to do with the information I have?"

A stranger's voice spoke from the door. "What information?"

The Godfather took center stage, became the lead actor in the game like he'd been classically trained.

"Jim Mallory. Come on over here you ugly ass duck."

Sheba watched the two bulls shake hands then tap their index fingers in some kind of tribal salute.

"Who's this pretty lady?" The pot-bellied, salami-smelling Italian queried.

"This is the Pin for my newly acquired Westside Region. Chandra Gully, say hello to my old friend Jimmy Mallory."

Sheba created lines for her part of the script, "Nice to make your acquaintance, sir."

"She's a classy dame, huh. A Black fox. You one foxy chick ain't you Chandra."

"Alright, back off, Jim-boy. She's spoken for."

Sheba noticed that Jimmy had a scar that ran the width of his neck. A Columbian necklace. Somebody had really gotten pissed off with Jimmy.

"Chandra, why don't you call me in the morning and we'll get things going. And for God's sake, take the bullets out of your piece before you show it off next time."

"Guilty as charged. I'll have everything ready for you. I'll keep the intel on that crawler in a safe place until you come back to work."

The farther she got from The Godfather's hospital room the better she could breathe. The fact that she was walking out of there meant The Order had believed her and The Godfather's story. But this nightmare was far from over. She had to find and face her son after she told him the truth about what he saw when he opened the door to her bedroom.

Nineteen

Raymond came barreling through the lobby of the ER with John Henry on his heels. When he saw Sheba he pulled her into his arms and held her there.

When he let go he said, "Why didn't you call me? I get home and this fool is posted up in the house with Diondre. The floor in our bedroom has blood all over it. What the hell is going on, Sheba? You let me come home to a scene like that?"

Sheba whisper-shouted, "Lower your voice! Let's talk about it in the car."

John Henry came over to where they were standing. "Sorry, She. Would've told him what went down but you told me not to say anything."

"Fine time for you to start listening to me."

Outside in the parking lot, Sheba asked Raymond, "How'd you find me?"

"The GPS in your phone. Sorry for tracking you but…"

"Where's Dee-dee?"

John Henry told her, "He was at home when we left. Told him not to leave until we got back."

As soon as they got to the car, Sheba tried Diondre's cell. It went straight to voicemail. She hung up and starting querying Raymond.

"How was Diondre acting?"

"Weird as hell. He was barely talking. He sat there staring at the wall like he was in a daze."

Sheba looked back at John Henry. She was relieved Dee-dee hadn't told Raymond what had gone down but she was worried as hell about how he was doing.

Raymond wasn't letting up. "I need to know what happened, Sheba."

"I don't want to get into a long…."

"I came home to blood on the floor of our bedroom! I need to know what happened!"

John Henry had to add his two cents. "Hey man, don't be yelling at her."

"John Henry…man…this is not the day for you to fuck with me."

"Look, I can't deal with you two at each other's throat right now!"

Raymond's expression let her know he needed concrete answers. "Sheba…"

"Okay. Fine. Here's the skinny version. The Godfather came over for dinner. He pushed up on Dee-dee's girlfriend. Dee-dee walked in on him. When Dee-dee saw him in our bed with Becca, he grabbed my gun. He was just gonna scare him. Then the gun went off and well….here were are. "

She prayed that Raymond would back down, that he would be satisfied with her tidbits of an explanation. He wasn't having it.

"What the hell was that animal doing in our bed with Dee-dee's girlfriend?"

John Henry butted in once again.

"Your *perfect* woman was two minutes from pimping out Diondre's girl so she could take her operation to the next level."

Raymond spun his head around back to Sheba and asked, "What is he talking about, Sheba?"

"You deaf? I said, your *wifey* set Diondre's girl up to be the fish on the hook for The Godfather. My boy came home early and crashed that party. Being the G he is, he had to teach that old dirty bastard a lesson."

Sheba threw the stick shift of the car into the park position while they were in motion. Darn near stripped the transmission.

"You know what, John Henry? Get the fuck out of the car. You always talking about what you don't know anything about. I know you're always hating on our relationship but this time you've gone too far. The Godfather wasn't even trying to get with Becca. He was testing her loyalty to Dee-dee."

"That don't have nothing to do with what you did."

"Rebecca texted me after she left. She said The Godfather never touched her. You don't know what the hell you're talking about."

"You need to calm down, Sheba. You're forgetting yourself."

Raymond's bullshit antenna was on full strength now. He knew something wasn't adding up.
"Why would he do that? Why would The Godfather think it was his place to test the loyalty of someone in our family?"

John Henry's gums started flapping again. "Because The Godfather…"

Sheba cut him off with a quick. "It really doesn't matter. It's over. Dee-dee is safe. The Godfather is alive. Becca didn't get hurt. And now *we* have intel on The Godfather that will keep *us* safe from here on out."

Raymond drove home in complete silence. When Raymond got quiet it meant he was really mad. And not just a little mad—he was finished.

When they got to the house, John Henry asked to come in and visit with Dee-Dee.

"Reach out to him in a couple of hours. He's been through a lot today."

"That's my son too. I have a right to see and talk to him just like you."

"Of course you do. I'll make sure he calls you."

John Henry grumbled over to his Lamborghini and cruised on down the driveway. Sheba raced for the door to find and talk to Dee-dee before he said anything to Raymond.

She yelled from the front door. "Dee-dee! Diondre, where are you?"

No answer. She went downstairs to the gym. Empty. She went upstairs to his bedroom. Nada.

She went down the hall to her and Raymond's bedroom. Raymond was in there packing a suitcase.

"Where'd Dee-dee go? Where're you going?"

"How in the hell does John Henry know the truth about what happened but I don't. I'm your man. You should've talked me first. I'm tired of playing second fiddle to a wanna-be-daddy."

"I was protecting you. Didn't want you to get caught up."

"Bullshit. What was he about to say when you cut him off?"

Sheba's eyes watered up. She sat down on the bed, saw The Godfather's blood and moved to a chair.

She blurted out part of the truth over a cascade of hot tears. "I can't....I can't believe Mama lied. All those years....nothing but lies."

Raymond sat down on the carpet next to her. "Sheba, tell me what's going on."

Tears pouring, her body shaking to the point of dang near convulsing, she told him what went down.

"I had downloaded all of The Godfather's financial data. I'm talking intel on his entire operation and the people he works for. I was about to take him out of his misery and use the intel as our ticket to freedom when John Henry tells me that The Godfather is my father."

"What the fuck!? John Henry's lying to you, Sheba. The Godfather probably told him to say that."

"Wasn't any money involved so John Henry had no reason to lie for The Godfather. There always was something strange about The Godfather and Mama's relationship. Something deeper than her knowing about the man he iced. I used to wonder why he did favors for me. Why he sent me birthday cards and Christmas presents. Even after Mama died. But I never looked into it because Mama said my father was dead."

"I always thought it was weird that The Godfather had just given you your own territory. Your fee hasn't gone up in years. No harassment. No strong arms. Nothing. What did The Godfather say?"

"He said John Henry was telling the truth. He also said John Henry used to work for him."

"What if The Godfather offered John Henry a piece of the territory in exchange for lying for him? I mean, he probably thought you were gonna take him out to keep him from retaliating against Diondre."

"John Henry isn't gonna do anything to hurt Dee-dee."
"He hurt you before. And when he hurt you, he hurt his son. He intentionally destroyed everything you built. You could've gone down behind his juvenile stunt."

"That was different. He did that to get back at me."

Raymond was mulling things over in his head. "If John Henry's telling the truth... maybe The Godfather didn't tell you he was your father because he was worried about your safety. That man has a lot of enemies."

"That's what The Godfather said. He said he didn't tell me to protect me."
"What else, Sheba? I feel like there's something you still haven't told me."

She started crying again.

"I did something....something Diondre might not ever forgive me for."

Raymond waited for her to spoon feed him the next serving of bitter truth.

"Dee-dee's best friend Fabian asked me for a job. I needed somebody on the street team. Somebody I knew would be loyal to me. He was green and I knew that going in. But he was hungry. I thought that would make him work hard. First day on the job he started running his mouth like diarrhea. Our competition overheard him talking about how we were taking over, how we were gonna own all the territory on the Westside of L.A."

"By competition you mean The Godfather?"

She nodded and finished the story.

"The Godfather and his henchmen picked him up. I had to bargain to get him released. I offered to cook The Godfather a gourmet dinner. During dinner, he invited me to take on some of his exclusive territory. When I tried to close the deal, he asked me to put a cherry on top. He wanted special time with Rebecca."

"I know you told him she wasn't for sale."

Sheba didn't answer—just shook her head back and forth like she didn't believe what she had done either.

"What did you tell him, Sheba?"

"She wasn't supposed to be there, Raymond! She said she was waiting on Dee-dee. That fool had given her his house key. Told her to wait for him to get home. I didn't have time to deal with her. I told her to stay in the back. She brought her fast ass out there and I couldn't....I didn't protect her."

She was balling again. Eyes were on swoll. Mascara running down her cheeks.

"You sure he didn't hit it?"

She blew her nose on the bedspread. "He didn't do anything to her."

"Becca corroborated his story?"

"Yep. She said he just asked her questions about Dee-dee."

"So you put Dee-dee's ace coon boon Fabian in the drug game. Then you pimped out Dee-dee's girlfriend to a Kingpin for a come up. Damn, Sheba. What the hell were you thinking? You won't be getting the *Mother of the Year* award will you."

"I was thinking that if I did this—if I pulled this off, I could get out the game for good."

"It might've cost you your son. I hope it was worth it."

"You gotta talk to him, Ray. Tell him something that'll convince him to forgive me."

"I don't know, Sheba. If it was me, if you were my mother, I'd be kicking your ass to the curb indefinitely."

"Just try. *Please.* Dee-dee's all I have in this world."

Raymond started to ask her what about him but changed his mind at the last minute.

"Go get yourself together. If you're okay Dee-dee will assume everything is under control. I'll call in a Cleaner to get rid of the DNA. Then I'll get somebody in here to fix the carpet."

"Ray, you know I love you, right?"

"Right now, at this very moment, I think the only person you're in love with is yourself."

Twenty

Sheba started with Rebecca then hit up all Dee-dee's friends. Somebody knew where her baby was and her wolf skills would help her track him down like prey. Rebecca's valley girl lilt answered on the first ring.

"He's not here Mama Ransome. He called me about an hour ago. He said he just wanted to make sure I was okay and that he was going out of town for a while."

"This is really important. I want you to think hard before you answer. Did he say where he was going?"

"He said he was going somewhere nobody would ever think to look for him."

"That's all he said?"

"Yep. He promised to be in touch."

"If he calls you, tell him he needs to get in touch with me. It's an emergency. Can you do that for me, Rebecca?"

"Sure Mama Ransome. That man you had over was weird. Like I told you earlier, he never touched me. Just asked me questions about Dee-dee. Like if I really love him and did I ever cheat on him. Right before Dee-dee bust into the room, he offered to pay ten G to sleep with me. I turned it down. All he did was smile when I told him no."

"Don't worry about that. In fact, let's never bring it up again, okay?"

"No problem. I'll call you if I hear from Diondre."

After they hung up Sheba thought about what Dee-dee had told Rebecca. That he was going somewhere no one would ever think to look for him.

She went through a mental list of places Dee-dee might go to hide out.

John Henry's house.
Fabian's crib.
Rebecca's spot.

John Henry would be elated if Diondre came to live with him. But Dee-dee also knew that would be one of the first places Sheba would look. Plus Dee-dee really wasn't feeling John Henry.

Fabian's spot was an option but Diondre knew Fabian and his mother were struggling. He wouldn't want to be a burden to them. Scratch.
Rebecca's parent's house was the logical place but Dee-dee wouldn't want to bring any drama there.

Sheba couldn't think of anybody else. She dialed Dee-dee's cell again. It went straight to voicemail.

*****

After they got the place cleaned up, Raymond said he was going for a drive. He was in the middle of temper tantrum and Sheba didn't have the energy to deal with it. She decided to let him get over it on his own like he always did.

By sundown she still hadn't heard from Diondre. Raymond hadn't returned either. When the phone rang she snatched it up hoping it was her seed. Instead it was him. The one God sent down to earth to test her.

"What's up, John Henry?"

"I called to talk to my son. His phone keeps going straight to voicemail. He at the house?"

She thought about telling him she hadn't seen their son since she stepped inside the ambulance with The Godfather but she already had a ton of fails on her marker.

"He's not here. I'll tell him to call you as soon as he gets home."

John Henry heard the stress in her voice. "You au'ight?"

"I'm good. A lot on my mind. But I'm staying strong. Being that wolf Dorothy raised me to be."

"You keep being strong, She. Our son needs you."

"Our son needs both of us."

That statement gave him reason to pause. "What's going on, Sheba? That nigga stressing you?"

"Like I said, just have a lot of my mind."

"When you're a wolf, you can't let the small stuff get under your fur."

"I hear you. But sometimes it's not that easy."

"Brush it off your shoulders like lint. You hear me, She? Snuff out your enemies. Leave some of their blood on the concrete so the other sheep'll know not to cross the line."

She chuckled and told him, "That your pep talk?"

"Gangster psychology 101." John Henry told her laughing.

He lightened her spirits just a little.

"I'll tell Dee-dee to call as soon as he gets in."

When she hung up she thought, *Problem is, I have no idea where Dee-dee is…*

Twenty-one

For the first time in twenty years, forty-eight hours had gone by since Sheba had seen or heard from her son. She couldn't sleep or eat. Felt like she was under a cloud of depression. Soon as the sun touched the horizon she called on her street team to help find her Dee-dee.

She had seven of them on a conference call. They were shocked when she told them the assignment.

"Today, you all have a different assignment. I need you to find my son. There's a big bonus for the person who delivers my package. Ten G. Cash."

From the rocky bluffs of Venice Beach to the polished halls of UCLA, they searched. In crack houses and dope houses, bar rooms and basketball courts—they looked and asked questions. The team that worked Dee-dee's campus had a picture of him. They shoved it in front of any and everybody he'd ever hung out with.

While the street team did their work, Sheba's shiny black Expedition pulled up in front of the crumbling steps of Fabian's Mother's house. The driver got out and knocked on his door. A few minutes later, Fabian sauntered down the steps. He was shirtless. His pants were sagging low, dangling at his hip bones. Sheba hadn't seen or talked to Fabian since he'd been relieved of duty at Ransome Industries. Sheba lowered the passenger window and met eyes with the one who'd kicked off a shit storm in her life.

"Mama Ransome. I'm sorry 'bout what happened. If you give me another chance I..."

Sheba lifted her right palm. "I'm not here for that, Fabian. I'm looking for my son. Have you seen or heard from him?"

Fabian looked up and down the street like he was checking to see if somebody was watching.

"If I have intel for you, what's in it for me?"

"You selling information to me? After all I've done for you? After you flapping your gums almost cost me my operation?"

Fabian pursed his lips, crossed his hands over his genitals and spread his legs into a thugly pose.

"I'm in a situation, Mama Ransome. As you know, I lost my job a week ago. I'm low on paper. Gotta get my mama's medications. They ain't cheap."

Sheba slid her hand into her purse, pulled out three crisp one hundred dollar bills. She held the money between her index and middle finger like it was bait.

The gum flapper started chattering. "Dee-dee called me this morning. Said he was at a spot somewhere off Canon Drive in Beverly Hills. He said...."

Fabian paused, rubbed his thumb and middle finger together. That meant he had more information but it would cost her extra.

Sheba pulled out two more c-notes and added them to the wad.

"He was mad as hell. Ain't never seen my boy that lit up. He said was gonna take you down. Is it true Mama Ransome? Did you pimp out Dee-dee's girl? That was some gangster shit if you did."

Sheba bit her lip to cover up the pain.

"Is there anything else?"

He rubbed his fingers again. "There's one more thing."

Sheba stuck another hundred between her fingers. Fabian looked down at the wad and licked his lips.

"I don't have all day. Talk."

"He thinks it's your fault that these addicts are hooked on phonics. And you know she carrying his seed right? His lil' shorty. Becca. He tell you yet?"

Sheba swallowed, invoked her inner wolf and went into Queenpin mode.

She tossed the money out of the window like it was trash. "You just forfeited your membership in the Ransome Queendom. I hope it was worth it. Have a nice life."

"Awww Mama Ransome. Don't be like that."

She lowered her glasses, looked at him with venomous eyes and said. "Don't *ever* call me that again."

She rolled up the window while he rambled on.

"Mondel, take me to Beverly Hills. 777 Canon Drive."

Mondel had been her driver for almost a decade. He had been driving the Kingpins of L.A. twice that. Mondel, like everybody in their industry, knew that was The Godfather's address.

He also knew no one dared go to The Godfather's castle without an invitation.

"Miss Ransome...um....you want....want me to call ahead for you?"

"I don't need to call. He has my son. I'm gonna bring him home.

Twenty-two

Submerged in the warm, sparkling waters of The Godfather's Jacuzzi, Diondre reflected on the life altering events that led to the moment at hand.

Five hours ago he'd stood in front of the Beverly Hills Police Station contemplating snitching on the Drug Empress of Southern California.

Sheba Ransome. His mama. His birth capsule.

The woman who cooked for him, changed his dirty diapers and nursed him when he was sick. The one who would take a bullet or even kill for him if it was necessary.

The same woman who was ready to turn out his girlfriend to come up in the game. The same mama who put his childhood friend on the street to sell her poison.

He was nine years old when he figured out his Mother sold drugs for a living. He'd heard her talking on the phone to one of her mules. She sat him down and talked to him straight. Told him people were going to use drugs whether she sold them or not. Said the authorities let drugs into the country and that they shouldn't be the only ones benefitting from them.

He asked her why she couldn't get a regular job. She justified her employment choice with the goal of wanting to save enough money to retire somewhere beautiful and warm while she was young enough to enjoy it. She said she wanted to send him to college without worrying about money.

He was a kid. All he saw was designer tennis shoes, trips to the Hamptons, chefs and butlers, the mansions they lived in. He never saw the pregnant mothers who got addicted to the product his mother sold or the babies in their wombs that were born with defects. He didn't see the families whose lives were torn apart when a dealer got busted. He knew nothing about the people his mother had ordered beaten or killed because they stole from her or tried to take her territory.

After overhearing her and his father's conversation, he'd packed a bag and headed for the door. Not only had his mother lied to him, she had intentionally put his girl in danger. It wasn't enough that her drugs destroyed the lives of people on a daily basis. Her team of me mentality has seeped into her own home.

Diondre had never lived on his own. He was used to having drivers and chefs, maids and tutors to help him navigate life. Now he was a part of the homeless population of South Cali. The first night he'd crashed in the dorm room of a friend. He knew his mom was looking for him so he skipped class the next day and staked out in a local coffee house. Depressed and confused, he'd sought shelter in a matchbox apartment in the heart of the hood where his homie Gerard lived.

He and Gerard went to high school together. Gerard—who now went by the nickname Kite—had just gotten out of jail. Diondre knew his mom would never think to look for him there. Not in one of the neighborhoods she had helped corrupt and destroy.

Kite lived off Hyde Park and West Blvd, near Inglewood, a few miles from a historic venue called the *Great Western Forum*, the place that made Kobe and Shaq a household name. Diondre had shaken his driver about a mile from there and taken the bus to Kite's house. That's when he got a bird's eye view of the world his Mother helped create.

His awakening started when two crack addicts solicited him as he walked down Hyde Park Blvd. One of them was tweaking bad. She had a screaming baby strapped to her back. She offered to take Diondre in the alley and blow him for a ten spot. Just out of curiosity, he asked her what she would do with the baby.

"He can't see nothing from back there. He ain't even gon' know what's going on."

Diondre had pulled out a fifty and tossed it to her. Then he realized that was probably a mistake. Fifty would keep her high all night long. Her baby wouldn't get any care while she was smoking. He choked back the tears and kept walking.

Two blocks later he saw a dealer being courted off to the pokey. Two little boys and a woman he assumed was their mother stood on the curb crying while their daddy and her husband was handcuffed and pushed into a black and white.

When he hit Crenshaw Boulevard he realized he was dressed totally wrong for this part of town. He snatched off his Rolex and stuffed it in his pocket. He pulled his baseball cap down over his eyebrows and yanked his shirt out of his pants. He was wearing six hundred dollar Nike sneakers but there was nothing he could do about that.

Nobody answered the first time he knocked on Kite's door. A few seconds later a little girl flung the door open.

"Hi Mister Man. You want five or ten?"

He was about to tell her he wasn't there to buy anything but someone inside started screaming at her for opening the door without permission.

"Bitch, are you crazy? Don't ever open my door unless I tell you to," the woman told her.

A full-bodied woman with a thousand-dollar hair weave and way too many diamonds for late afternoon pushed the little girl back so hard she slid across the hardwood floor on her hind parts.

"Who you here for?" The ratchet feline demanded.
"Here to see, Kite. It's Diondre." He tried to sound tough but his voice squeaked.

The woman looked him up and down and knew immediately he was neither a customer nor was he from their part of town.

"You five-o?"

Kite came up behind her. "Back up, Mama. That's my nigga, Diondre! What up, mein!"

Kite's mama shouted, "Lil' Diondre?! We ain't seent you over here in years. Nigga, where you been? You was doing time in the pokey?"

"Be cool, Mama. He just got here."

Diondre and Kite did the Black man handshake, bumped chests and pointed at each other.

Inside the apartment there were kids everywhere. Two in cribs in the living room. Five of all different ages eating Mickey Dees and playing with the toys that came inside the box.

Four men sat at a card table playing cards, smoking blunts and drinking beer. All of them were strapped with the latest artillery. An elderly woman was stretched out on a tattered couch watching something violent on a widescreen TV. There was a pipe laying next to her on the couch. Her air was being piped in through an oxygen tube that was hooked up to a dust-covered breathing machine.

Kite invited Diondre to an unoccupied corner of the living room. He pointed to two flimsy folding chairs. Diondre took a seat while Kite went to the kitchen and came back with two jars of red Koolaid on ice. He handed Diondre a jar and sat down beside him. Diondre tried to ignore a roach scaling the wall next to where the older woman was laying.

Diondre flashed back to high school. Him and Kite under the bleachers by the football field tongue kissing shorties. Stopping at Save-on Drug Store for Metropolitan flavor ice cream cones. Hitting *H-Salt Fish & Chips* for some of that greasy fish smothered with tartar sauce, vinegar and ketchup.

"Man, remember when you made that bank shot and won us the regional championship?"

Kite smiled proudly, "Hell yeah, I remember. That was the best day of my life."

"Why you didn't play ball, man? I'm just saying. You were better than all of us."

"When Moms got caught up with the drugs I had to quit playing ball to help take care of my baby sister. Got me a job at McDonald's. That shit was hard on a nigga. By the time they took out taxes, mein, I barely had enough to buy some kibbles and bits. That's why I started slanging. Then I got busted. Lost two years of my life. But I'mah get it all back. Be like you in a minute. College balling and shit."

"Let me know what I can do, man. My family knows a lot of people. You moms—she clean now?"

"Yeah, mein, she just smoke a little weed and get her a beer on Fridays. It's all good. So what you been up to Dee? Where them bitches at? I heard you balling out of control. I just got home so you know I'm ready to get my swerve on."

"Man, ain't shit happening. Going to school. Trying to get a contract. Dealing with some drama with my moms."

"You know you can stay here, man. It's a little crowded but I got you, homie."

"Thanks man. You know what, Imah call my mom's driver and we can roll to the club. Platinum passes and bottle service—you know how we do!"

"Hell yeah, man. Let me change clothes and take a quick shower. You wanna chill in here?"

Diondre looked around. It was a war zone in the living room.

"I'll come in the back with you."

They headed for the bedroom in the back of the house.

Kite asked him, "Ey mein, you ever talk to that that big booty chick you used to fuck with in high school? She got like eight kids now."

Before Diondre could answer, the gates of hell opened up. The front door got kicked in. He didn't know if it was the police or a gang hit.

The men at the card table went for their pieces. When the shooting started, Kite snatched a gun out of his boxers and shoved Diondre into the bedroom. As Diondre stumbled backwards into the room he saw one of the little girls take a bullet to the chest. Kite screamed for Diondre to get out of there as he slammed the door and went to war for his people.

Diondre heard the exchange of gunfire erupt on the other side of the door. Terrified, his eyes darted around the bedroom searching for a way out. He scrambled to his feet, dove out of an open window, hit the ground and rolled across the wet grass.

When he looked up, he was eye to eye with a snarling pit bull. Luckily the dog was on the other side of the fence. Heart pounding, he stepped up with his right foot then flung his body over the fence in one swoop and ran toward the alley. He didn't stop running for ten blocks. He rushed into a liquor store, hid behind the aisle with the chips and Ho-ho's, pulled out his cell phone and called his mom's driver.

Mondel got there in seventeen minutes. It was one a.m. and he had been asleep when Diondre called him but he did his job like he always did.

It wasn't the first time Mondel had to rescue Diondre from an unsavory situation. But this time was different. He could've lost his life back there. Diondre was hysterical when he flopped down onto the back seat.

"You alright, man? What's going on?"

Mondel was a big guy with a kind face. He had hands the size of baseball mitts and skin the color of midnight.

Diondre was in a rage. "It's all her fault! One of my best friends is probably dead because of her fucking drug business!"

"What you talking about, Diondre? What happened?"

"They just shot up my boy's house. Killed one of his little sisters."

"Who shot them up?"

"I don't know. It was bad. Real bad. I almost got killed."

"You want me to call your father?"

"Hell no. He's part of it too. Need to get in touch with Raymond."

"Auight, man. Calm down, okay. You're safe now."

Diondre dialed Ray's number but it kept rolling straight to voicemail.

"Just take me by the house. He's probably sleep and has his ringer turned down."

Fifteen minutes later he was rolling through the front door. The house was dark, everybody was out. His mom had left him a note saying Raymond was at his Mother's house and to call her when he got home. Dee-dee had Mondel take him by Raymond's mom's house. Raymond knew something was wrong when he saw Dee-dee at the door that time of the morning. After Raymond calmed him down, Diondre told him the whole story starting with the day he shot The Godfather.

"It wasn't your fault, man. None of it. Your mom wasn't thinking. I'm sure she wasn't going to let The Godfather mess with your girl."

"I heard her tell Dad what she did. I can't forgive her for this one."

Diondre and Raymond always had deep conversations and tonight was no different. Raymond confided in Diondre that he had been thinking about breaking things off with his Mother.

"This is the kind of stuff that….that's why me and your moms might not make it, man. You and me, we cool. Always gone be cool. I love her but I'm getting tired."

148

Dee-dee begged him not to leave her.

"If you leave her, she's done. You're the only person in her life that loves her for her. The only one who doesn't want something."

"I can't make any promises but I won't leave while your moms is going through a tough time. And you already know you're my main man, to the last stand."

Early the next morning, Diondre was laying on the couch at Raymond's mom's house watching TV when breaking news chimed in. A newscaster stood in front of an apartment building off Hyde Park and West Blvd near Inglewood relaying the tragic news of seven murders. The next frame showed the bodies covered with white sheets including two children. It was a gang style murder over drug territory. His friend Kite, Kite's mama and family were dead. There was one survivor, the little girl who had answered the door. The newscaster said her name was Lakisha Carter. Turns out she was Kite's daughter. One thought went through Diondre's mind when he saw the bodies lined up on the grass covered by white sheets. *Sheba Ransome was going down.*

He didn't know how or when it would happen but he would see to it that his mother paid for what she had done.

He went down the hall and said his goodbyes to Raymond, grabbed his backpack and headed for the door.

"Where you heading, man?" Raymond asked without being pushy.

"To see a friend."

"Be careful out there, Dee-dee. A lot of wolfs on the prowl looking for their next meal. Don't make me have to take one of them down over my son."

Dee-dee smiled when Raymond called him his son. And then he thought to himself, *if only my father treated me like that....*

Twenty-three

Diondre hadn't known Raymond wasn't his father until he was seven years old. His dad had come to by visit him when he overheard him telling Raymond that he had no right to say anything about what he told *his* child to do. That's when he found out that the visitor who came by every other weekend was actually his father and that Raymond—the man who cooked, helped him with his homework and took him to school every day—was his Stepdad.

Diondre didn't want John Henry to be his dad. Not then and not now. John Henry looked, dressed and talked like a gangster. He made a ton of promises that he never kept. Not only did he not show up for their scheduled visits, he didn't even have the decency to call.

Raymond was smart as hell and he was always there when Diondre needed him. When Raymond he came to his school, he dressed like a business man. His schoolmates always commented on how nice Raymond dressed. Some of them thought Raymond was his dad. Diondre didn't correct them.

The day Diondre shot The Godfather, he'd come home excited. Couldn't wait to tell his mom and Ray about how he'd slam-dunked on those ballers. His team was in line for a national championship. He also had some other big news he was going to tell her. His high school sweetheart Rebecca was pregnant.

When he saw Rebecca in bed with that bastard, he lost it. He thought The Godfather was trying to rape her. After he shot that sorry excuse for a human being his Mother sent him

151

down the hall to clean himself up. He was coming back down the hall to see if the old geezer had checked out when he heard his parents talking about what had really happened and why.

Bottom line, his mother was a liar and a thief. She'd done horrible things to innocent, unsuspecting people. Somebody had to stop her. He thought maybe God had picked him to be the chosen one.

A few days later he made the call to Detective Zion Justice of the LAPD. He met Detective Justice at a Career Day on campus a few months before. At the Career Day, Diondre heard people calling the Detective by his last name. *Justice.* He'd asked him why they called him that. He told him it was because when he took on a case, he went after the perp like a beast. And he didn't give in until he got what he came for—justice.

Diondre had been nervous as hell when he punched in the digits from the business card Detective Justice had given him.

"Is...Detective Justice around?"

"This is Justice."

"This is Diondre Ransome. I met you at the Career Day at my school. I play ball."

"Yeah, the baller—I remember you. Whassup man? You trying to trade in your sneakers for a uniform?"

Diondre almost hung up. But he'd come too far to turn back.

"Actually…I'm calling you about other business."

"Okay."

"I got information on a drug ring. Financial records. Bank deposits. Info on where the product is being stored and sold and…."

Justice interrupted him. He knew the phone lines weren't secure. "Can we talk about this in person?"

"Yeah, I guess so. I can be there in a couple of hours."

"Have the front desk ring me when you get here. Don't talk to anybody else but me. Understand?"

"Yep. I'm gonna send you an email with some files in it."

"Alright. I'll look for it. You have a number where I can reach you?"

Two hours later Diondre stood in front of the police station with enough intel to bury his mother. He opened the door and locked eyes with the officer working the counter.

The officer shuffled a few papers around on the counter, tried to look busy. After a few minutes, he looked up and asked, "What can we do for you?"

Twenty-four

"Nothing. I'm in the wrong office."

He had changed his mind about snitching for one reason. Raymond. If the cops went after his Mother, Raymond—the only real dad he had ever known—was going down too. He couldn't let that happen. Not after all he'd done for him. He'd have to think of another way to destroy his Mother. One that wouldn't hurt Raymond.

A long, black limousine was parked in front of the precinct. Diondre figured it was his mother. He'd heard she had been looking for him. When the back window of the limo rolled down Diondre realized it wasn't his mother—it was the man he'd shot a few days ago with his mother's gun.

He walked to the bottom of the steps, stared angrily into the old man's eyes and yelled, "What the fuck do you want?!"

The Godfather would've killed anyone else for talking to him like that. He swallowed his rage and remembered what this was about—protecting his daughter.

"I need to talk to you, son. It's about your mother."

"Fuck her and fuck you. And I ain't your son. I don't wanna hear shit about her. I was gonna let it all go but seeing you...knowing all the shit that you and my mother have done—I gotta go handle this."

Diondre turned around and headed back up the steps to the police station.

The Godfather called out to him. "There's something you need to know before you make a decision you can't undo."

"It's over. I'm taking her and anyone involved in her operation down."

"Five minutes is all I'm asking for. I'll leave you alone after that."

Diondre stared at the double doors leading inside the police station. Two more steps and it was done.

He wondered if The Godfather knew something important?

He thought maybe his sorry ass father had sent him. But he didn't want to hear anything that fool had to say either.

Diondre glanced up and down the street considering his options. He could get in the car and hear what The Godfather had to say or go through those doors and make it all go away.

Once again his love for Raymond made him walk back down the stairs and get into the limousine. His granny had always told him there was two sides to every story. Maybe The Godfather knew something that would change his mind.

They drove in silence to The Godfather's luxury condo in Beverly Hills. After a short tour, The Godfather's butler escorted Diondre upstairs where he took a hot shower and put on some swim trunks. The Godfather had his chef prepare a delicious lunch of broiled steak, steamed broccoli and mash potatoes. When they were through eating, Diondre followed The Godfather outside to a monstrous Jacuzzi.

The Godfather stared off into space as his feet dangled in the steaming water. Diondre slid down into the water a few feet away from him and exhaled. After a few minutes of awkward silence, The Godfather broke the ice.

"I never meant you, your mother or your grandmother any harm. If you let me explain—I think I can make things clear."

"I'm listening."

"When it came to business, your Grandmother was a wolf. When it came to the people she loved, she was a lamb. She wanted me to give her the American dream—husband, kid and a white picket fence. Tried to explain that I couldn't give her that life. I had power but not enough to get out of the game. If I had tried to leave back then they would've killed me and anybody I was close to."

"Grams told my mom you were dead. That you had died broke and she had no way to taking care of us."

"Your grandmother always did have a colorful imagination."

"I don't understand—why would she lie about it?"

"Dorothy didn't want her daughter looking for me. And she was pissed because I wouldn't leave The Order and marry her. She didn't understand—those who got out had lots of money to pay for their freedom. I'm talking millions. And you have to get out of the game for good because when you leave The Order, you lose their protection. That means the other side—their rivals—are coming for you. They want information. If they can't buy you, they'll kill you. So you have to leave the country or live the rest of your life looking over your shoulder. And I had a good reason to stay in America."

"So why'd you kill that guy? The one Grams covered for you?"
"Who told you about that?"

"I heard my mom and dad talking about it."

"He said he was gonna touch my daughter—your mother—when she was a little girl."

Diondre looked him in the eyes like he was seeing him for the first time.

"What you mean, *touch?*"

"You know what I mean. Fucking pervert threatened to touch my little girl inappropriately. I had to kill him."

"Why would Grams get mad at you for taking out a man like that?"

"The man who did it--he was one of her best clients. He had brought her thousands of dollars of business. She asked me to let it go so I did. Then I saw him at a bar not too far from your Granny's place. The bastard started joking about it. Said Sheba was a little freak that needed taming. I waited for him to leave. Followed him to his house. When his driver dropped him off, I jumped out of the car and pumped four rounds into that fucker. Then I spat on him and pissed on his forehead. Pedophile didn't deserve to live."

"How'd they find out you did it?"

"Somehow a button came off my jacket. Cops found it when they swept the murder scene. They did a search of my house and found the jacket it came from. They charged me but they couldn't convict me on a button. Since there were no witnesses, it came down to my whereabouts on the night in question."

"Grams told them you were with her."

"Yep. She saved me. But not without a price. Whatever your Grams did for somebody always came with a price tag. In exchange for her vouching for me, I had to promise to never tell Sheba I was her father.

Diondre was about to ask him why he didn't just marry her and let the chips fall where they may but the butler interrupted them.

"Sir, there is a visitor."

"Who is it, Johnny?"

"It's the boy's mother, Sir."

Diondre grabbed a towel and exited the Jacuzzi. "Tell her lying ass to come on in. I got some questions for her."

The Godfather stopped him, "Hold up. Stop right there. Sheba might've made some mistakes but that's still your mother. Don't ever disrespect her in this house."

"Fuck that! People are dead! Babies are born addicted to the shit she sells. Somebody has to hold her accountable."

"That might be true but this isn't the place nor the time. Are we clear?"

The Butler waited for a cue from The Godfather on what to do about Sheba.

"Are we clear, Diondre?"

Diondre nodded his head. The Godfather said, "Okay, let her in, Johnny. Have her wait in my office."

The Godfather gave Diondre a glare that let him know he was still a wolf, a wolf with sharp, deadly fangs.

"You need to calm down, son. You're acting like a boy—that's not the way men handle things."

Diondre shoved his hands in his pocket, slowed his breathing down a bit.

The Godfather led the way to his office, the room where he did everything from negotiate million-dollar drug deals to execute enemies.

As they walked, The Godfather explained the significance of the space they were about to enter.

"I call this room the nucleus because it's the center point of my operation. This is place where kingdoms rise and kingdoms fall. Your mother was conceived in this room."

The Godfather opened a big glass door with a polished brass handle. Sheba was seated in an oversized white leather chair near a window that looked out over Beverly Hills. She stood when she saw Diondre, rushed over to hug him. He didn't push her hands away but he didn't respond either.

"Why didn't you call me back? I was worried as hell. You could've at least let us know you were okay."

He felt The Godfather's eyes on him. "A lot on my mind."

"What you doing here?"

"Talking to my grandfather."

Those words made Sheba's stomach turn. She was still trying to get her mind used to the fact that The Godfather was her father. The Godfather explained the circumstances that had led to her son ending up at his address.

"Our intel gave us heads up that your son had a meeting at the police station."

"That's how you knew where I was?"

Diondre was blown away.

"Told you we have eyes and ears everywhere."

"I want you to leave my son out of this. He has a chance for a life that we never did. Let him go."

"I'm not holding him here, Sheba. He can leave anytime he wants to. He was about to take the law into his hands. Was trying to keep him from making decisions there was no coming back from."

"What kind of decisions? What do you mean—take-the-law-into-his-own-hands?

"Diondre, you want to tell you Mother what you were about to do?"

Diondre looked down at the floor and told her, "Yeah. I was about to turn you in and take down your operation."

The bottom of Sheba's stomach dropped out.

"You were going to the police on *me*—your mother?"

"My *mother* pimped my girlfriend to move up in the game. My *mother's* drugs got my boy's entire family killed. Then my *mother* broke the, "no-family" rule by hiring Fabian, my broh from another muh, to deal for her."

She poked her index finger into his chest and told him. "I carried you in my womb for nine months, endured twenty-six hours of labor and you were going turn me in to the cops? And for your information, my *drug business* fed and clothed your ungrateful ass. It's the reason you go to the best schools, wear designer clothes and live the lifestyle your *boy* came to me begging to have a piece of."

"Correction. I'm *gonna* turn you in to the cops."

The Godfather got in the middle of them. "Nobody's turning anybody in."

"I already did. I emailed the detective files from her computer."

Sheba's heart started pounding. "You did what?"

"You heard me right."

Diondre hadn't realized the enormity of what he'd done until that moment.

"You....you silly, selfish ass little boy...."

Tears rolled down her face.

"You have no idea what you've done. They'll take everything from us! Other people will be implicated. They'll come after you too. They won't stop until we're not breathing."

The Godfather pulled out his phone to see if anyone had texted or called him. There were no messages. That was a good sign.

"Let's calm down and think this through. Son, I need to know exactly what you sent the police."

Diondre was crying now. "I didn't mean to....I was just trying.....All I knew was she had to pay for what she's done!"

"Well, we're all gonna pay. Me, Raymond, your dad-- everybody!"

"Sheba! I need you to calm down. We're gonna figure this out."

Sheba paced back and forth. "I need to call Raymond. The police are probably on the way to the house with a search warrant."

She went into crisis mode. Texted everybody in her operation with the code for two hour clean up. They knew what that meant. All hard drives would be destroyed. Laptops would be dumped into the ocean. Sim cards gathered and burned.

Sheba called Raymond and told him what Diondre did. Raymond went silent for ten seconds. She thought he might've hung up.

"Raymond? Hello? You there?"

"I'm here, Sheba. Maybe this is for the best. Your money's safe. You have most of it in off shore accounts. Maybe you should just throw in the towel and keep it pushing."
"I'm not going talk about this over the phone. Right now, I need to get rid of the hard drive in my office computer."

"I'm burning it now. I know the drill. Anything else?"

"There's a significant amount of cash in the safe in our bedroom. My jewelry is in there too."

"I'm putting it in the holy place."

Sheba knew he was talking about the drop box she'd installed that was buried fifty feet underneath the house.

"Raymond, you need to get out of there. They'll be coming soon. Take the two paintings—the ones that belonged to my mama—from the living room. I love you."

"I love you too. We'll get through this."

When she got off the phone, The Godfather motioned her over to his desk. She couldn't even look at Diondre. She wanted to tear his head off his body and stab him a thousand times but she loved him too much to lay even a hand on him. She made him invisible—put him in a non-existent place in her heart and mind.

"Diondre gave me a list of the documents he emailed. Let me ask you a question. Are your computer files encrypted?"

"Of course they are. But if they have real people—real techies—they can break the codes."

"I might have someone who can help you. He's a master at scrambling files. In the meantime, if they take you in, don't admit to anything. And don't let them pressure you into plea bargaining."

Sheba logged onto Dee-dee's laptop, opened the tools and put in the password for the encryption device. She handed the laptop back to The Godfather. The Godfather picked up a red phone and five seconds later somebody named

Bones came in the room. A few seconds after that, somebody named Black went to work on Dee-dee's computer.

When he was done, Black turned to them and said, "Unless they're NSA, ain't nobody downloading those files."

Sheba thanked them both and headed toward the door.

"I have to get home now. Time to face the music."

Before she walked out of the door she said, "I hope you're happy, Diondre. I hope you accomplished what you set out to do."

She walked over to The Godfather and put her arms around him. It was the first time in her life she had hugged her father.

The Godfather swallowed the lump in his throat that stood in between the tears rushing to his eyes.

"Take care of yourself, Sheba. I'll be in touch.

Twenty-five

Balding men in cheap suits drifted from room to room tagging and bagging potentially incriminating papers from Sheba's drawers and cabinets. Their faces were expressionless as they went about their work. Her freedom made it clear they hadn't found anything worthwhile. Yet...

Sheba sat down on a stool in the kitchen and waited for the man in charge to come over and talk to her. An hour later, agent number 1621 sat next to her and tried to exchange some dry humor.

"You want to confess and get this over with? You could get a good deal with a plea."

"I have no idea what you're talking about. I can't say anything without my lawyer present. Speaking of attorneys, do I need to call one?"

"Not yet but as they say, don't leave town."

After they were gone, Sheba called to check on Raymond. He was in Riverside at his brother's house. She wondered if Dee-Dee had gone with him but couldn't bring herself to ask.

"The cops just left. They ransacked the house. Took what they could. But there really wasn't anything that could cause a problem."

Raymond knew not to talk about anything on the phone. "You okay?"

They were speaking in code. She knew what he meant. He was asking if she was in danger.

"Yeah, I'm good. As good as someone can be in a situation like this. They told me not to leave town."

"Unless they have a warrant, they can't stop you from going anywhere."

"They can do anything they want. They're the cops."

Raymond was quiet for a minute then he said, "Dee-dee's upstairs sleep."

"Do me a favor. Don't mention his name to me right now."

"Sheba, he's just a kid. He didn't know what he was doing."

"He knew *exactly* what he was doing. And I'll never forgive him."
"You're right. Let's not talk about it right now."

"Look, I'll keep you posted. I'm gonna take a bath and try not to think about my own son trying to destroy me."

"It's gonna be alright. You want to come here or…you need me to come back?"

"Its best you're not here. Don't want you involved. We'll figure out next steps in the morning."

"I'm already involved. When I said yes to who I knew you were, I said yes to this day right here."

"I love you, Ray. But this…this is my mess. Call me when you guys get up. We'll do breakfast somewhere up that way."

She was in the bathtub soaking away the pain in her heart when the doorbell chimed. She assumed it was either Raymond or the cops coming back to take her in. When she turned on the doorcam, it was John Henry's towering body standing at her front door. She wrapped her wet naked body up in a robe and tipped up the stairs. When she opened the door, he walked right past her—entered her domain like he lived there.

She tightened the belt on her robe, realized she was as naked as she was the day she was born. John Henry kept his distance. He wasn't sure if Raymond was at home or not.

Sheba knew why he'd come. "You heard about what happened."

"Yeah. I heard about the weak ass shit our son did. I'll handle him when the time is right. Right now, we gotta do what we gotta do. You here alone?"

"Ray's at his moms. Dee-dee's there too. Let's not talk about anything here."

"Pack your bag. You're coming to my place."

She didn't have it in her to fight with him. She went to her bedroom, got dressed, threw some clothes, shoes and a few

168

toiletries in an overnight bag. On the ride to John Henry's place, she purged some of the pain in her gut. Let it explode like fireworks.

"While I was out there looking for him, while I was worrying myself to death—he was at the police station getting ready to rat on his mother. Does he even know or care why I went through all this shit? I did it for *him*. I did it so he wouldn't have to worry like I did. So he never has to think about where a meal is coming from or wake up to the sound of a trick banging some woman in the room next door. He went to the best schools, lived in beautiful homes. This is the goddamn thanks I get? Fuck him! And I mean it, John Henry. Fuck Diondre Ransome Henry—little ungrateful bastard can go straight to hell!"

She didn't realize she was crying until she stopped raging.

John Henry let her purge—let her get it all out. Then he told her, "Some punk ass shit my son did. He broke the universal law. You don't ever call five-o on family. Ever."

"I was wrong to let The Godfather sleep with his girlfriend. I was wrong to put Fabian on the street team. But I never did anything to intentionally harm our son."

"He looks at it like you sold him out when you pimped his little chippie."

"I messed up bad. I know I did."

Few minutes later John Henry put his palm flat down on a digital device at the entry to his estate. Security waved at him as he drove by. His black Rolls Royce glided up to the

169

door of a fabulous mansion that reminded Sheba of one of those exotic villas in the Bahamas. His second car—a cream colored Lamborghini—posed in the driveway making a clear statement to all his visitors. He was rich, he was Black and he was a man.

Sheba hadn't visited John Henry in years. They'd lived together years ago but it was totally different place back then. Now the whole place was state the art from floor to roof. John Henry was buying it, finally claiming a permanent place to plant his dreams and aspirations.

John Henry's home was nothing short of a woman's paradise. Soft colors, romantic lighting, elegant furniture—all designed to impress the ladies he brought home.

"Nice place, playa."

Her compliment was a subtle dig.

"Why I gotta be a playa?" He asked, flashing that hundred-million-dollar smile that made women drop their panties within minutes of entering his domain.

John Henry picked up a remote and with the flick of his wrist, turned on the fireplace and some mellow jazz on the stereo. A colorful aquarium filled with exotic fish lit up and almost hypnotized her.

"Make yourself at home, She. Mi casa, su casa. I'm gonna jump in the shower."

For a minute, Sheba imagined herself as the lady of the house. Holding dinners in the formal dining room. Laughing

170

with guests on the terrace while they sipped sparkling wine. The memory of the pain that came with that life ended her fantasy and brought her back to the present with a flash.

While John Henry showered, Sheba took herself on tour. She strolled down the hall to the kitchen and grabbed a bottle of mineral water from the sub-zero refrigerator. She popped in and out of the guest bedrooms, peeked in the media room, paused at her ex's state of the art gym. When she got to the master bedroom, she couldn't resist looking inside.

That was a big mistake. John Henry was just getting out of the shower. He had a towel wrapped around his lower body. His skin glistened with sparkling drops of water.

His manly fragrance dang near overpowered her—she had to snap herself out of it before she snatched that towel off and starting dining on his jewels.

She licked her lips. Played off how turned on she was by pretending she was looking for something.

"Uh…where's the towels?"

"Linen closet, across from the guest bathroom."

She turned around so fast she almost lost her balance.

John Henry chuckled a little and asked, "You okay?"

"Yeah, I'm good." She answered without looking at him.

The bastard knew full well what he did to women with his six-foot-two frame, caramel skin and bedroom eyes.

"You can sleep in here if you want to. I mean—we slept in the same bed for years. But if you're uncomfortable with it, there's two guest rooms. Take your pick."

He walked up behind her. Put his thick, tight body against her backside.

She spun around to face him. "Back up, John Henry. You know I'm in a relationship."

He backed up two inches. "You know we could be really happy together."

"Don't start or I'll be taking my ass home."

"Can a brother get a hug? You treat me like an enemy. I know we had our differences but we're still family."

"You can hug me after you put some clothes on."

He turned his back to her, dropped the towel and slid into some silk pajama pants. When he turned around, Sheba could see the imprint of his family jewels as clear as daylight at sunrise.

He opened his arms and she went to him. His body felt strong and familiar. That made her feel safe. Her tears came for the second time that day.

"How could Dee-Dee do this to me?"

"He was mad. You know how we Henry men are when we're pissed."

"I'm scared. I can't do jail—you know that."

"Ain't nobody going to jail. Don't worry. I got you, okay."

She wiped her face and walked off toward the guest room before she did something else that would devastate and destroy somebody she loved....

Twenty-six

"Is there a way I can drop the charges?" Diondre asked Raymond over breakfast.

"You haven't filed any charges. What you did was give the police evidence. You can choose not to testify against her but you can't take back the incriminating email you sent."

With regret in his eyes Diondre confessed, "When I saw Kite and his family get killed it messed me up. Kept thinking about Moms and how she put those drugs on the street. I started thinking that my family was somehow connected to what happened to Kite. That and what she did to Rebecca— got me twisted.

"No way of knowing who Kite's family was selling for. There's hundreds of drug dealers in Cali. But you're right. Indirectly, your mother's business supports the systems that keeps drugs and violence in our communities."

"How you deal with it? I mean, that's your woman."

"When we first got together—when I found out what she did for a living—I had a decision to make. I chose to stay. So I can't walk around acting brand new or like I didn't know this was a possibility and neither can you. I don't need her money or the material things it buys. Never did. But your mother...she likes to live a certain lifestyle. And it's not cheap. I've been trying to get her to retire for years."

"I'm not saying I forgive her. But she's my Mom Dukes and I can't let her go out like that."

"You might not have a choice now. How you dealing with knowing The Godfather is your Grandfather?"

"I don't trust him. Probably never will. But you know that man he killed back in the day was a child molester. The Godfather said he was trying to mess with mom when she was a little girl. That's why he took him out."

Raymond had always felt something bad happened to Sheba.

"I'm real sorry your Mom went through that."

"The Godfather took care of it. I got love for him for handling that."

"Well, there's other ways to handle crimes like that. We can't just go around killing people who do wrong."

"That pedophile deserved to die."
"I hear you, Dee-dee. And I understand how you feel, man. But we aren't God. We have no right to judge and condemn His people. That's what courts are for."

"The court lets animals walk free every day. You know he would've abused other children."

"Like I said, I hear you son. But when we as citizens start taking the law into our own hands, where does it stop? And how do we keep it from being subjective?"

"What you mean by subjective?"

"Subjective means how something is viewed through the eyes of an individual."

"Child abuse is wrong no matter who is doing it."

Raymond decided to let the discussion go.

"You wanna go see your mother?"

"Yeah. I need to go by my Dad's too. Left something in his car that I need for school."

"Get dressed. We leave in 30 snaps."

Twenty-seven

Sheba's car was in the driveway but the house was completely dark. Raymond went to enter the code into alarm system then realized Sheba had forgotten to arm it the night before. He and Diondre walked through the property in silence, like they were breaking into a stranger's house.

Raymond's voice was hushed. "Your mother's probably asleep. I'll wake her up. You go grab some clothes. I'm gonna put us up at a hotel for a few days until this thing blows over."

Raymond called out to her once, twice. No answer.

Diondre came back to the living room with a small gym bag and his backpack in tow.

"Where's ma?"

Raymond tried to hide his concern. "Probably at the office already."

When Sheba's cell went straight to voicemail Raymond got even more worried. Thought maybe she'd been taken in. He sent her a text. She called fifteen long minutes later.

"Sorry it took me so long to call. Just waking up."

"Had me worried for a minute. Where are you? I'm at the house and...saw the bed hadn't been slept in."

She lied. "Yeah, I got a room last night. Just didn't feel safe at home. Passed out soon as my head hit the pillow."

"Why didn't you take your car?"

"Limo dropped me off. Didn't feel like driving."

"Meet us for breakfast?"

"I...I'm not sure I'm ready to breathe the same air as Dee-dee right now."

"I'll drop him off and come meet you."

"You two go ahead. I'll catch up with you later. I just need a minute to think."

"We'll get through this. Love you bae."

"Love you too."

Raymond hung up with an uneasy feeling. His spidey circuit had lit up and he wasn't sure why. Sheba's voice had a slight fever of nervous energy. She was explaining herself a tad too much which was out of character for her normal whose-gives-a-shit attitude.

He figured maybe she was wired up because of what had just gone down with the cops. But the feeling that he was standing on the edge of a cliff with Sheba behind him wouldn't go away. He decided to talk to her about it later.

Dee-dee jumped in the car and they headed over to John Henry's house to pick up whatever he had left there. Raymond considered calling Sheba back to see if he could get to the bottom of the mystery but decided against it. He'd just have to wait until the truth unfolded. Fortunately, it always did. But what Raymond worried about was, sometimes the truth was like a shotgun blast to the middle of your chest. And when that fire hit you, you didn't know if you would survive or perish in the flames…

Twenty-eight

"Turn right at the light. Then pull up to the security gate."

Raymond and Diondre were pulling up to John Henry's estate. Diondre planned on talking to his father about how to handle what he did.

In all the years he and Sheba had been together, Raymond had never visited John Henry's home. Sheba told him that John Henry had upgraded their digs—that the new house was totally different than the one they lived in. It didn't matter. Until then, he had refused to step foot on the land of a man who had once bedded his woman.

When they pulled up to the guard station Diondre told him, "I have to put my hand on the fingerprint reader."

Raymond wondered why John Henry had his place on lock down. Guard tower, fingerprint recognition box, cameras in the trees lining the long driveway to the front door. Maybe it wasn't the contents of the house but the man who lived in the house he was trying to protect.

As they reached the top of the hill, the front door opened. Raymond almost drove into the bushes when he saw them.

"What the hell? What the fuck is Sheba doing here?"

Diondre was as speechless as Raymond was when he looked up and saw his mom standing on the steps.

John Henry had his arm around her waist. Her Louis Vuitton overnight bag was in his other hand. Sheba was laughing about something. They looked like they were starting their day after a long pleasant night.

Raymond threw the car in park. Dang near stripped the transmission. His feet hit the pavement before the wheels stopped rolling.

Sheba stopped in her tracks when she saw Raymond and Diondre.

Raymond walked up the steps toward her and John Henry. He looked in Sheba's eyes and told her, "You lied to me."

"Raymond, I'm so sorry. I just….just needed to get away."

"Over here? To this nigga's house?"

Diondre shook his head in disbelief. "Such a liar."
"What did you just call me?". Sheba's hand was hot enough to slap the taste of out his mouth.

"I called you a liar because that's what you are!"

Sheba tried to grab him by the throat but he dodged her hands.

Raymond shook his head back and forth. "This is the shit I can't deal with."

John Henry went into warrior mode.

He dropped Sheba's overnight bag on the steps. "You ain't gonna disrespect me and my son's mother on *my* property, in front of *my* son. I'm not trying to get in y'all's business, man. But this can't go down up in here."

"Fuck you and your house, John Henry. You've been disrespecting me the entire time Sheba and I have been together. Saying inappropriate shit. Pushing up on her. Don't think I didn't see it. I didn't check you because of your son. But shit has gone too far."

Sheba tried to deescalate the situation. "Raymond, give me a chance to explain."

"Explain what? How selfish your ass is? How you only think about you—what you want and what you need? I already know. I've been living with it for 10 years. Tolerating your lies and outbursts—the games you play with other men that you pull into your web of deceit. It ends today, Sheba."

"Raymond, I love you and only you. Nothing happened last night. John Henry heard about what happened and came by to check on me. When he found out I was there alone, for safety reasons he invited me to crash at his place until the morning. That's it."

"That's not the point, Sheba! You lied to me. You let me find out like this instead being woman enough to tell me the truth."

Frustrated, Sheba yelled, "Everybody lies, Raymond! It's what people do."

Diondre eased back up the steps next to Raymond.

Raymond shook his head. "Not people who love and care about each other. When people love you, they tell you the truth, even if it hurts."

Sheba burst into tears. "I'm human. I make mistakes."

Sheba's tears made Raymond soften for a minute. He went back to being hard a few seconds later. He wasn't letting her off the hook this time.

"This wasn't a mistake it was a decision. There's a difference. You made a decision to lie to me about spending the night at your ex-husband's house."

"Nothing happened! I swear on my mother."

"Something did happen. You lied. The truth matters, Sheba."

"Just let me explain. I…"

"Save it." He turned to Diondre. "Dee-dee, you staying here, man?"

"Naw, I'mah roll with you."

John Henry bucked up one final time.

"You gonna leave your father and your mother standing here to go with him?"

Diondre puffed his chest out, stood toe to toe with the matador.

"Raymond's been more of a dad to me than you ever have and probably ever will be. He's the one who taught me what a parent is supposed to act like. Maybe you and mom could figure it out if you weren't so busy trying to con and swindle people."

John Henry lunged at Diondre but Sheba jumped in front of him.

"John Henry, stop!"

John Henry shoved her to the side and got in his son's face. "Boy, you ain't gonna stand on my steps talking to me like you crazy. I'm still your father. Regardless of what you think about me, I'm the one that gave you life. Not him."

Raymond jumped in front of Diondre. John Henry pushed him back so hard he almost fell down the steps.
"Watch out, Raymond!" Sheba reached out to grab him and block his fall.

Raymond's feet were tangled up for a few minutes. He twisted his body around and got his footing back. When he was upright he stared John Henry down with pure hatred in his eyes. "The only reason this isn't going down is Diondre. But I'll be coming for you. Word is bond."

John Henry balled his fists up and banged them on his chest like he was a King Kong. "Come on! Bring all you got! You know where to find me. And you better come packing. I lay 'em down and pray over 'em when I get through whooping that ass."

"Stop it!!! Both of you just stop all this craziness!" Sheba screamed.

Diondre was crying when he said, "Any man can make a baby but it takes a real man to be a father. Weren't you the one who told me that, Dad?"

"Get the fuck off my front porch. You are no longer my son."

Diondre and Raymond headed for the car. Sheba ran after them.

At the car she told Raymond. "I'm going with you. Take me home."

"Seems to me you *are* home."

John Henry carried Sheba's bag over the car, opened the back door and tossed it on the seat. Sheba plopped down next to it and slammed the door without a word.

"Don't bring this drama to my house anymore. You hear me, Sheba?"

"Whatever, John Henry. You came to *my* house remember? Next time, stay your ass home."

He shook his head back and forth. "You know what....be glad our son is here...."

"Or what? You gonna beat my ass too? I dare you to put your hands on me!"

"I never said I was gonna put hands on you. I would never hurt you, Sheba."

"Whatever. Let's go, Raymond! Get me out of here."
"Don't be yelling at me—I'm not one of your chauffeurs!"

"Just get me out of here. Please."

Twenty-nine

The ride home was cryptic, not a word between them. Diondre broke their non-talking spell with a confession.

"I was wrong, ma. I'm dropping the case. Gonna tell them I screwed up. That I got everything twisted."

"That window is closed now, son. Damage has already been done. We shut down Ransome Industries yesterday. Burned everything it took years to build."

"What? Dang Ma….I….I never meant to….well, maybe closing Ransome isn't the worst thing in the world. Maybe it was supposed to happen."

"Yeah? Guess I'm *supposed* to owe a lot of powerful people a shitload of money. And I have to make good on those debts even if my business is closed. And if I don't pay…."

Sheba paused to look at a call coming through on her cell.

"You know what? Let's drop it. Nothing we can do about it--so what's the point. And we can't talk about this inside the house. Not until I have my guys come in and do a sweep of the entire property."

"One more thing, Ma. My laptop is missing. Thought I left it at Dad's house but he said it's not there. Last time I had it was at The Godfather's place."

"I have it. You forgot to get it back at The Godfather's people did the encryption to scramble any messages or files you sent out over the last seventy-two hours."

"Did it work?"

"We'll know in the morning. The feds haven't indicted me yet—so that's a good sign."

Diondre was quiet for a minute or two then he told her, "I gotta go to practice. Missed two days already."

"That's good. Going to practice makes you look normal. But call the driver and have him take you. Don't want you out alone right now."

Raymond still wasn't talking. Sheba tried to feel him out.

"Raymond, can you call the Cleaners for me?"

He knew she was referring to a group of specially trained men that clean up evidence at the homes and offices of people who do illegal business.

"Told you I already did. But after this, I'm done doing your dirty work, Sheba. I'm just here to pack my stuff."

When they got to the house, Diondre headed for the pool house to shower and change clothes. He'd learned at a young age to get ghost when grown folks were beefing.

Sheba and Raymond went to their massive bedroom. Raymond carried on in silent mode as he tossed clothes in a suitcase and packed up his essentials. Sheba curled up in a fetal position on the bed and watched her future prepare to become her past.

When he finished packing, Raymond hopped in the shower. A few minutes later he walked out naked except for a towel around his lower body. He sat on the edge of the bed and rubbed a fragrant balm over his chiseled body. Sheba loved the smell of a freshly bathed man and found herself getting turned on. She slid out of the bed onto her knees.

"Please don't leave. I'm begging you, Raymond. I can't get through this by myself. I never begged anybody. But I'm asking you….asking you to do this one last thing for me."

She put her hands on his knees. Buried her head in his lap. Let her tears baptize his legs. Raymond put his hand on the side of her face. Traced the outline of her chin and cheekbones with his fingertips. Sheba moved her face around in his lap until the tip of his manhood was poking her through the towel. She eased her hand under the towel and stroked until she felt it throbbing in the creases of her fingers. She kept her head down and eyes closed feigning full submission.

She massaged his love like a sculptor creating a masterpiece. She inched her face close enough to slide it into her mouth. Gave him pleasure in measured doses. Got him close to exploding then backed off to let the tension build. She used her lips and tongue to work him to a frenzy then drove him into home plate by licking and slurping until he released a long, powerful orgasm.

When she finished dining on his nectar he made her lay back on the bed. Without a single word, he slid her black pants and purple panties down.

Pressed his tongue against her opening. He used his tongue to sex her down. When she was ripe he gave her his index and middle finger. Softly sucked her pearl while he worked her G. Let her come like that just to take the edge off.

Then he mounted and rode her until she exploded like a wave onto an ocean shore.

"Ohhhhh...Goddddd! Coming so fucking hard for you baby. This. Is. Your. Fucking. Pussy. Fuck me, Raymond! Coming all over your dick right now!"

Raymond loved how raw she was in bed with him. How vulnerable she was when he was inside of her. He came again. Let his seeds fill her up to the brim.

When they came back to the earthly dimension, Sheba told him, "I was wrong for not telling you where I was. I was all messed up inside. Feeling alone. I knew Dee-dee was with you and I just couldn't face him yet. But nothing happened. I swear on my mama's grave nothing happened."

"I already knew that. But that doesn't excuse you lying to me. This thing with you and John Henry....I know he's still in love with you. But what pisses me off is that you allow him to hang on like there's hope. I guess he's your ace in the hole. Problem is, I don't play those kind of games. Somebody always ends up hurt."

"Read my lips, Raymond. I don't want John Henry. If I did, I could have him."

"You get off on men falling down over you. Flirting gets you high."

He kept talking but he wasn't talking to her anymore. He was talking to himself.

"Pleasing you is like trying count the grains of sand on the beach. Like trying to carry water in a basket. A man could be standing there with his throat cut, arteries hanging out and you'll be telling him how he forgot to pick up milk on the way home."

"What are you talking about, Raymond. I give my all to you. I fuck you the way you wanna be fucked. I suck your dick the way you like me to suck it. I buy you the things you've always wanted."

He kept talking out loud to himself. "You're like candy to a diabetic. Even though we know the shit is probably gonna kill us, we just keep on eating."

"Fuck you, Raymond. I never forced anybody to do shit. Ain't nobody being held captive by me who doesn't want to be a prisoner."

"Now that's the Sheba I know and love."

She threw her hands up in the air and told him, "What do you want from me? You knew who I was when we met. Told you I was a wolf. I showed you my fangs. Scratched you with my claws. Now you want me to act like one of the sheep. It's not gonna happen. Sheep get slaughtered. They trust the shepherd to protect them and end up getting shanked and turned into lamb chops. Not me. Not this bitch."

"You might have to lose it all to appreciate it. What you already have will never be good enough. It's always about that next new thing you're trying to get. You want us to be your pets—sniveling at your ankles waiting for a doggy treat. I'll never be your bitch, Sheba. That ain't me and it never will be."

"Men are a fucking trip. It's okay if they whore around, sleep with multiple women, have two, three different baby mamas. It's alright if they make career moves at the expense of their wives or girlfriends. But if a woman does any of the above she's a selfish bitch."

"I never asked you for a damn thing. Most men would've walked long time ago. I'm not a fool or a trick. I did it because I love you. And I love our son."

Sheba's eyes were filling with tears. "I know what I have in you. One of the best men God ever made. A good man who loves me for me. Not my body. Not what I can do for him. *Me.*"

"Then act like it. Stop letting the outside world disrespect me."

"What the fuck are you talking about, John Henry!"

Sheba gasped when she realized what she'd called him.

"Wow. You had my dick in your mouth twenty minutes ago and now you're calling me another man's name."

"We were just talking about him and I slipped."

"Why don't you just fuck him and get it out of your system. Maybe that'll help you figure out what you want to do."

"I don't want to fuck him. I just want to love you and have you love me. I want us to be happy."

"Happy? You wouldn't recognize happy if it bit you on the ass. We had everything, Sheba. Beautiful home. Happy kid. Successful businesses. Great sex. You focused on what we didn't have. Guess it doesn't matter now. It's all irrelevant. What I know is this—I will no longer share my present with your past."

"What are you saying, Raymond?"

"I might not be all hip, slick and city cool. But I carry respect for you no matter where I am or what I'm doing. And no woman, man child—nobody—can make me compromise the love I have for you. That's what I'm bringing to the table. And that's why I need back from you. I need you to decide, Sheba."

"Decide what? He's the father of my child—he's always gonna be a part of our lives."

"You know what I'm talking about. He comes by here to see *you*, Sheba. This isn't about his son—hell, he barely spends time with him. I see the way he looks at you. How he drools when you walk into the room. Read my lips. I'm done sharing you with your ex."

"I hear you, Raymond."

"Look, I'll be back in a few hours. I'll stay around until you get through this legal situation but I'm making no promises after that."

Thirty

After Raymond left, Sheba made herself a cup of cocoa and curled up on their massive bed. She exhaled and inhaled the smell of the sweet love her and Raymond had just made. She wished he was there to hold and comfort her like he usually did after they had sex. But he'd left her there to lament over the sins of her mother and the ones she'd committed herself.

The events of the last few weeks slammed down on her like avalanche. Tears welled up in the pit of her stomach, moved up her to her throat and poured out of her eyes. She decided to let them fall. She needed a good cleansing.

After the tears were emptied, her mind went to mama. Miss Dorothy Ransome, AKA the Alpha Wolf. She thought about how her mama had programmed her. How she'd made her believe that life was all about getting paper and being on the winning side of the chessboard. Sheba had followed her advice to the tee. She'd buried her emotions in a deep hole

and worked hard every day to keep them hidden from anyone who made her even think about being weak. But now the advice Mama had given had nearly cost her everything

that meant anything to her.

Sheba remembered a conversation she and Mama had on her sixteenth birthday. Mama had taken

195

her to the Sizzler Restaurant, the one across the street
from The Great Western Forum. Sitting at *their*
table—the corner booth near the emergency exit—
Mama counseled her on the way a wolf lives and moves.

      "We're wolfs, Bethsheba. We kill, eat, mate and travel
to find new prey. The only ones we're loyal to are the
members of our pack."

      "What if we become friends with a wolf from another
pack?"

      "The only true friend a wolf has is their own cubs or
their parents."

      "I've read stories about wolves taking in trade from
other packs."

      "With complete submission. Even an alpha wolf has to
bow down to the leader of the more powerful pack. That's the
law. Bow down or be devoured. Sometimes the alphas fight to
the death to prove who is the strongest."

      "Did you have to fight other wolves, Mama?"

      "Every day I fight off a wolf that wants to take over my
pack and claim my territory."

      "Why you call them prey?"

      Her mother was getting irritated by the questions.
Sheba could see it. She backed down as her mother answered
the last question from that day's Wolf Training Class.

"Some men are born marks and probably gonna die marks. That's why we call them our prey. They're tricks, Sheba. And tricks want and need to be tricked. You gotta get them before they get you. You hear me girl? And remember, all men cheat. But the more you get from 'em the less likely they are to leave you for the chippie they're cheating with."

The table had been stacked with boxes. Sheba had nodded her understanding of her Mother's wolfology then started tearing open boxes. There were designer purses and shoes, the latest electronic gadgets, a tennis bracelet with matching diamond earrings, tickets to Disneyland and Magic Mountain. Sheba was so excited she could barely breathe.

"Mama, where did all this stuff come from?"

"Most of it comes from my customers. The bracelet and earrings are from me."

Dorothy's customers knew the way to her heart was through her daughter. On Sheba's birthday they went all out.

"I don't even know them."

"They know your mama. That's good enough. There's one more thing...."

Dorothy slid a small black box from her purse. Set it in the middle of the table.

"This right here....this is special. This is gonna set you apart from all those little chippies at your school."

"What is it, Mama?"

"Open the box."

Inside the box was a car key bearing the Mercedes Benz insignia.

"Is this what I think it is?!!"

"Go outside and see."

Sheba ran outside just as a black Mercedes with tinted windows rolled up to the curb. It had a big pink bow on it.

"It's yours, baby. A good friend of mine sent it over for you. I call him your uncle. Uncle Simon."
Sheba knew better than to question her but she couldn't believe a customer had given her mother a forty-thousand-dollar car.

"Mama, what did you do to get Uncle Simon to buy me a car?"

"What I tell you about questioning me? Look, let's just say I know some of his secrets. Secrets that he wants to keep buried until he ain't breathing no more."

That was the day Sheba decided to become a wolf. A boss. A queen bee. An alpha wolf just like her mama. A modern-day Nino Brown who ruled her Queendom mercilessly.

What Sheba didn't understand was that her mother's life hadn't been as glamorous as she made it appear. Mama

Dee had been a loner for years. She was bitter and callous. Her soft womanly parts were buried under the pain of her unhealed childhood. She had passed those scars down to Sheba under the guise of getting money.

A ghetto celebrity, when her mother died only a few people showed up to the funeral. They had to hire people to carry her coffin to the gravesite. Sheba didn't even know the minister who did her Mother's eulogy. It was a sad life when you knew so many people when you were alive yet the people at your funeral were mostly strangers.

Sheba had been raised to believe no one could be trusted. Raymond taught her that wasn't true. Raymond wasn't perfect but he was trustworthy. She knew for a fact that his love was sincere. He'd never given a damn about who she was or how much she had in her bank account.

John Henry, on the other hand, was just the opposite. He was always on the hunt for the next best thing. A finer woman. Somebody with a higher status. Everything, including the people he loved, was disposable and replaceable. Just like Sheba's mother, John Henry pretended he needed no one and cared about nobody. But it was all a cover for how wounded and afraid he was on the inside.

Sheba's mother had used her daughter to get ahead just like she used the men in her life. Sheba was a pawn on her Mother's chessboard—proof that somebody had cared enough about her to knock her up. Sheba was her doctor, her lawyer, her friend and confidant. Sheba made Dorothy seem human in a world that had no humanity.

Dorothy parented Sheba the same way she ran her whorehouse—with an iron fist and satin glove. When Sheba needed a hug, Dorothy bought her something. When Sheba got an A on a test at school, instead of congratulating her, Dorothy used it as a way to get money out of her marks. Mamadee accepted perfection and nothing less.

If Sheba got into an argument with a kid a school, Dorothy had one of her henchmen rough up the child's father.

Her mother never asked if the argument had been her fault. Even though Sheba was a good student and could've gotten good grades on her own, Dorothy paid the teacher to give her nothing but A's.

It didn't take much to set her Mother off. Sheba learned very young how to keep her Mother calm enough to get what she wanted. Sheba played a mind game. She pretended she couldn't live without her.

"Promise me you'll never leave me mama. Who would take care of me if you left?"

"If you don't stop getting on my nerves I might just disappear without a trace. But if something happened to me you'd go live with one of my father's sisters down south."

"But I don't know those people."

"If you acting up, what happens to you ain't my problem. I'll just adopt me another daughter and leave her all my riches."

Sheba didn't know if she was serious or not. And she didn't want to find out.

This was the programming she had taken into the relationship with her son and with Raymond. The belief that she could buy her way out of anything. That people were disposable. That rich people didn't have to be accountable for their actions.

What she'd done to Diondre was wrong, dead wrong. Not money, status or anything else would make it go away. She had to find a way to make things right.

Sheba thought about Diondre and Rebecca expecting a baby. They were so young—too young to become parents. But since they had already made a decision about their baby, there was nothing Sheba could say or do.

Sheba's mind went back to the battles in her present. Staying out of jail. Paying off a hundred and fifty thousand dollars in drug money. After she won that battle then she had to get her man back and get her son to forgive her. She also had to learn to live with The Godfather being her biological father.

It was a lot to handle but one thing Dorothy's tough love had taught her was how to survive. Mama always said there was a back door to every room. Sheba would just keep on turning doorknobs until she found the door that opened up to freedom.

Thirty-one

Sheba needed something to lift her out of the funk she'd
been in since Dee-Dee had turned on her. She drove up
Crenshaw Boulevard to a small Black burb in Los Angeles
called Leimert Park. She swung a right on 43rd and turned
into the driveway of *Cleopatra Hair Salon & Spa*. She dropped
a C-note on the receptionist and got an appointment on the
spot with Medusa, their top braider. While she was waiting for
the Queen of all things braided, a woman with long thick locs
sashayed through the reception area. Sheba noticed her deep
eyes and wide hips as she strolled past her. The woman wore
multiple strings of colorful beads around her neck. Large
brass Ankh-shaped earrings dangled from her ears.

The mystery lady stopped in front of her and stared
into her eyes like she wanted to say something. Sheba started
to feel a little creeped out so she asked the woman, "Do I know
you?"

"No. We've never met. But I saw something when I
walked by you and…."

"Saw something like what?"

The woman paused as if she was listening to someone
talk in her ear.

"Let me ask you this—do you believe that people can
see into the future?"

Sheba laughed and told her, "Yeah, my bill collectors
can see that if I don't pay the light bill they're gonna cut off my
lights."

"You believe in psychics? You know, people that know things before they happen?"

"Most of them are just con artists preying on innocent people but I guess there's a few real ones out there. Forget all the small talk—is there something you want to tell me? I mean, are *you* a psychic?"

"Yes, I am."

"Good for you. I'm not interested. No disrespect but I prefer to let things play out."

"You might not want to do that in this situation."

Sheba's mother had consulted psychics, tarot readers and everything in between. One of her mother's employees told Sheba that was how her mama picked numbers for the horse races. But Sheba had always relied on her own intuition and as far as she was concerned, it had worked just fine.

"I appreciate your concern Miss....what's your name?"

"I'm Violet. Violet Brown."

"As I was saying Miss Brown, I appreciate your concern but I'm a very successful business woman. I don't need a psychic to tell me what works for my operation."

"This isn't about your business. This is about your son and your husband to be."

The mention of Dee-dee made Sheba shiver. She hadn't told the woman she had a son. And technically, her and Raymond weren't engaged. But if the woman knew something that could help her get through this crisis, it wouldn't hurt to give her a chance.

"I tell you what, I have fifty dollars and fifteen minutes. Can you work with that?"

"I don't want your money. I just don't want to see you go down a road you can't come back from. Why don't you step into my office."

Sheba swallowed hard and followed the woman next door to a little store that had incense, candles, tonics and tinctures on display. In the back there was a small table covered with an indigo colored cloth. There were crystals and other paraphernalia on it. Sheba sat down at the table. She was still skeptical but was a tad bit more open to hear what the woman had to say.

"Would you like some water?"

"No thanks. Please go ahead. I don't have much time."

"I have a message from someone with a D name."

Sheba swallowed hard. "Man or woman?"

"Woman. Older. Big hips and long black hair."

"Go on."

"She wants me to tell you not to make the same mistake she did. The woman—the one with the D name—says because of the way her mother treated her, she never trusted anybody. She was afraid to love and afraid to be loved and therefore couldn't teach you how to love."

"You're talking about my mother."

Sheba fought back the tears. She didn't understand how this stranger knew so much about her mother. And she never knew her mother's mother had abandoned her mama. Mama told her that Annie—that was her gran's name—had died of a heart attack.

The psychic continued. "She's saying something about the Wizard of Oz?"

Sheba's heart started pounding—she was sure the psychic woman could hear it.

"Her first name was Dorothy."

"I see. Who's the little boy with the D name?"

"Shit. That's my son."

The tears rained down her face. Sheba went in her purse and pulled out a fifty.

"Can I get ten more minutes? I have a couple of questions."

Miss Brown nodded.

"Is Raymond coming back to me?"

Violet paused, looked somewhere over the horizon and told her, "Not to you—not to the woman you are now. But if you change, he'll give you another chance. Stop lying to him and stop treating him like....like a client. He'll come back. He loves you. I mean he *really* loves you."

"I know he does. Second question. Will my son ever forgive me?"

When Sheba asked that question the tears cascaded again. Miss Brown paused and gave her some tissue before dropping a bomb of an answer.

"He already has. But you have to stop trying to buy his love. Out of guilt for being who you are, you've spoiled him. Instead of teaching him to value who he is, you taught him that his worth was tied up in possessions. Its gonna take a little undoing but it's not too late for him to evolve."

"I'm all messed up ain't I?"

"You're not messed up. You just have some work to do. Your mama did the best she could with what she was given. She missed a few classes in the parenting school. But you're a survivor. You're gonna get through this."

"Thank you, Miss Violent. I apologize for what I said earlier."

"Don't worry about it. Keep in touch. There's more you need to know but in due time."

"Do you have a card?"

Thirty-two

On the way home, Sheba stopped by her office which was as quiet as a morgue. So different than it was just a few weeks prior. She drifted through the empty halls of Ransome Industries down to her corner pocket that overlooked a cloud-covered city. She sat down at her desk and called the one person who always knew how to fish her out of muddy water.

"Ronnie, it's me. Sheba. I need you to come up for air for a minute. I have a real emergency. Money is no object."

Sheba expected to hear back from her friend and former employee within minutes. After an hour had gone by she texted her a follow up message.

"Ronnie. Its serious. Diondre's involved. Call me on the red phone."

Sheba knew if Ronnie heard her mention the Red Phone and Diondre in the same sentence she'd understand the seriousness of the situation. Plus, Ronnie was crazy about Diondre and Sheba knew she'd fly out of her batcave if she thought something was wrong with her Dee-dee.

Two minutes later, the phone rang.

Ronnie had been among the lucky ones who had gotten out of Sheba sticky's web before it destroyed her. Ronnie told Sheba that her and her girl crush were doing good. They were planning on going on one of those Rosie O'Donnell gay cruises to the islands.

"So you've made a mess of things and need your clean-up woman to sweep up the trash. It was Diondre's homeboy Fabian wasn't it? Tried to tell you that kid was trouble but you didn't want to hear it."

"Ronnie, you know how much I hate I told you so's. This is bigger than Fabian. But the bottom line is, you were right and I was wrong. I fucked up. I admit it."

"Because I love that son of yours, I'll do what I can."

Sheba told her all of what had gone down, except for the part about The Godfather being her father. She was keeping that information very damn close to the vest right now.

"I hope the potential come up you sacrificed it all for was worth it."
"It wasn't. And we can't do shit about the past so let's stop talking about it."

"Don't get mad at me because you were being a shallow ass, power hungry, money grubbing Queenpin."

"Damn, say exactly what's on your mind why don't you. You've become a little crass while you were on sabbatical."

"Penelope's been helping me with speaking my truth. She says I hold in way too much and that's why I have heart problems."

"What's wrong with your heart?"

"Nothing that a little heart medication, a low carb diet and a stress-free schedule won't cure."

"I see. Well, after you help me with this, I won't bother you anymore."

"It's not like that. I care about you. I've always cared about you. But I was just a phase in your life. I don't want to be anybody else's emergency plan. I have my own life now."

"You were there for me when my heart darn near stopped beating. You healed me. You made me believe in me again. I'll always owe you for that."

"Those words mean a lot to me. But you don't owe me nothing."

"They're not just words."

"Sheba, you know I don't do mushy. Let's get back to the business at hand."

Sheba took a sip of her mineral water and continued.

"I need to set up a company. A construction company."

"Real or dummy?"

"The real thing. We have the bricks and mortar building. Now I need the brains, heart and kidneys. Can you help me with that?"

"Of course. You need back records?"

"Yes. We need to be in business for three years."

Ronnie took out a small notebook and wrote a few things down. "What kind of work we do? Build office buildings, add-ons for houses—what?"

"The whole nine yards."

"How many people work here?"

"Fifteen or twenty including the construction workers to start."

"Got it. I'll make it all legit. I'll also work on getting you a few real clients."

"Thanks, Ronnie. I really appreciate you."

"Take care of Diondre. You're all he's got."

"His dad is there for him."

"Like I said, you're all he's got."

Sheba's eyes misted up a bit. "A lot of hurdles to get over huh? At the end of the day I just want to be happy. I don't want to worry about wars or territory anymore. I don't want to go to bed thinking about the harm my drugs are doing to the community."

"First time I ever heard you ask for that. All you ever talked about was getting money, getting a man and getting some more money."

"Don't get me wrong, I still like money. And I love me a fine ass, good smelling man and a good ass orgasm. But I've come to realize there's a couple of things that are just as important."

"Like?"

"Family. Security. Trust. And loyalty—loyalty can save your life."

"Yes it can, Miss Ransome. Yes it can. For now, let's get back to resurrecting your company and making you legitimate."

Thirty-three

It was midnight when the first call came in. Sheba was in a deep sleep. Dreaming about the Fiji Islands and one of those hotels that are built right on the ocean. She heard the phone buzzing but thought it was coming from some distant place in the land of slumber.

Fifteen minutes later, the phone buzzed again. Sheba turned over and peeked at the screen to see who was blowing up her phone in the middle of the night.

John Henry. Who else.

She turned around and looked over at Raymond. He'd finally come home, back to her bed. Last thing she needed was to get caught talking to John Henry in the middle of the night.

Fifteen minutes later John Henry rang her phone again. It was the third call in forty-five minutes. That meant something was very wrong. John Henry was crazy but not that crazy. Sheba tipped out of the bed, made her way upstairs to the kitchen and called him back.

She whisper-yelled, "What's up? You better need a kidney calling me in the middle of the night."

"I was at a party on the East Side. This little Latin chippie told me there's a contract out on The Godfather. Five million pesos to the first Merc to send a picture."

"Shit."

"Don't get in the middle of it, She. Not your war, not your fight."

"Gotta let him know. That's the least I can do."

"Knowing him, he already knows. But I'm telling you because I don't want you and my son getting hit with a stray bullet."

"Your Latin bombshell—she say who or why they're after him?"

"They think he might snitch."

"Damn. This is happening because of what our son did to get back at me. When he went to the police station that day, The Godfather showed up. They probably thought he had something to do with Diondre narcing on Ransome Industries and that he was gonna snitch on them too."

"Whatever the reason is, stay out of it. Like I said, not your war."

"Actually, it is my war. I started the ball down this path. Now I gotta stop it from hitting the wall."

"She, don't…."

"I gotta go, John Henry. Thanks for the heads up."

Thirty-four

Sheba called The Godfather six times back to back. Texted him the same number of times even adding a nine-one-one code. When he didn't answer, she got worried that the Mercs had already found him. If they hadn't got to him she had to find him before they did.

She thought about waking Raymond up to tell him what was going down but figured she'd just drop in on The Godfather and be back before her man woke up.

She wrote Raymond a note and stuck it to his cell phone screen. It was short and to the point.

Hitmen are out to get The Godfather. He isn't picking up. Driving over to Canon Drive to give him heads up. Back in forty-five.

She jumped in Raymond's Lami and hightailed it over to Beverly Hills. When she got to the entrance of The Godfather's building, she called him again. No answer.

She used the special remote he'd given her to get into his drive-up elevator. She pulled her car inside and felt the rush as it jetted her to the sixth floor.

The Godfather's goons let her in and pointed her to a rooftop Jacuzzi where her seed giver was chilling with his flavors of the week. When he saw Sheba coming through the door at that time of the night he knew something was up.

After he dismissed his chippies and poured himself a glass of champagne he asked,

"So what's going on, Bethsheba?"

Hearing her full name spoken the same way her mother used to say it threw Sheba off for a minute. She quickly regained her composure and told him why she was there.

"They're coming for you. Real deal killers. Been texting and calling you."

The Godfather seemed unmoved. Like she'd just told him an old friend was stopping by.

"I was…was a little preoccupied."

"Yeah, I see."

"How did you get this intel?"

"John Henry called me. He was at some party on the Eastside."

"How much is my life worth on the streets?"

"Five million pesos."

"Two-hundred and fifty thousand American dollars."

"That means they got some bonified mercs on your trail."

"Yeah, I heard you the first time. And you risked you and your son's safety to give me a heads up?"

Sheba started crying. She wasn't sure why but something deep down in her soul felt sad, angry and scared.

"I guess….guess I'm not ready for you to die."

The Godfather's eyes told her he was moved.

"Don't worry. It's not my time."

Before she could ask him how he knew that they heard gunfire erupt from the lower rooms.

"Somebody doesn't agree with you!"

The Godfather grabbed her by the shoulders and shoved a set of keys into her hand.

"I want you to take these keys, go through that red door, press the number six on the keypad and wait for me on the roof. If I'm not there in twelve minutes, get on the helicopter and tell the pilot to take you and your family to 333."

"What's 333?"

"Don't worry about it. He knows."

Just as Sheba made her way across the room toward the red door, glass from the windows surrounding the patio shattered from gunfire.

The Godfather screamed, "Get back over here. Follow me!"

Sheba ran back across the room and followed The Godfather through another door that led to a secret stairwell. They ran, jumped, half fell down the stairs. The door at the bottom of the stairwell led to a parking structure.

Dressed in swim trunks, house shoes and a blue terrycloth robe, The Godfather pushed Sheba behind him as they eased through the parking lot door and inched along the wall toward a red Porsche. He pressed numbers into a pad on the door handle. The car doors unlocked and the vehicle's engine roared to life.

The Godfather threw the passenger seat back and pulled open a hidden panel. He slid out two guns and a box of bullets. He gave one gun to Sheba and stuck the other one in the waistband of his swim trunks. He dropped the bullets into his robe pocket and surveyed the perimeter.

Sheba was crouched on the ground next to the car. The Godfather was about to tell her to go around to the passenger side when he saw a monster truck burst through the security gate and burn rubber up to the level they were hiding out on.

"Get down!" The Godfather told her as he dropped to the ground behind the car, cocked the gun and prepared for battle.

They heard the vehicle stop and the sound of footsteps moving across the pavement. The Godfather eased his head up and saw John Henry standing next to a yellow Humvee with his cell phone out. Sheba's phone starting playing the Nicki Minaj *Truffle Butter* ringtone associated with John Henry's phone number.

"Sheba! Where you at?!"

Sheba rose up and peered over The Godfather's right shoulder.

"John Henry? What you doing here?"

The Godfather said, "This isn't the time for twenty questions. Let's move!"

The Godfather and Sheba ran for John Henry's vehicle. Sheba got in the front and The Godfather slid into the back seat next to John Henry's Latin bombshell.

"Sheba, The Godfather, meet Consuela. Conseula meet Sheba and The Godfather."

The woman became hysterical in a matter of seconds. "What the fuck is going on, Shon Heenry? You need to take me home right now! I didn't sign up for this shee-it. Your stoo-pid ass is not gonna get me killed tonight."

More gunshots rang out from inside the apartment.

Ignoring her rantings The Godfather yelled, "John Henry, get us the fuck out of here."

"Where to?"

"Hangar 310. Private airport on Prairie and 120th."

John Henry burned rubber out of the parking lot and to the street.

When they were sure no one was following them The Godfather made a few calls to arrange for their flight out of hell.

Sheba called Raymond. He answered on the first ring.

"Where in the hell are you? I woke up to a crazy note and my woman M.I.A."

"I don't have time to explain. I just need to you get Diondre and meet me at the airport."

"What the fuck is going on?"

"If you want to live, leave the house now. That's the situation."

Raymond started tossing clothes in an overnight bag. "Damn, Sheba. You must have trouble tattooed on your ass. What airport are you talking about?"

"Hangar 310. A little private airport off Prairie Avenue and 120th. Google it! Just get your ass off the phone and in the car with my son."

"Diondre has company. What should I do with his girlfriend?"

"Bring her ass or leave her there. I don't give a damn."

Raymond hung up, ran downstairs and woke up Dee-Dee and Rebecca. He told them to pack a bag and be ready to leave in ten minutes. Next he called Sheba's driver. By the time him, Diondre and Rebecca flew out the front door, the driver was outside with the car doors open waiting to whisk them off to safety. Mercs pulled up to the house five minutes after they drove off.

At the airport, Sheba, The Godfather, John Henry and Consuela were sitting on The Godfather's plane. The Godfather kept checking his watch and the window every two minutes.

"Shon Heenry! Let me off this plane!"

"I already told you I can't do that. Everybody saw you leave with me at the party."

The Godfather was getting tired of her cackling. He tossed John Henry a roll of duct tape. "Can you shut her up?"

John Henry put a strip across her mouth then added a second one for good measure.

The Godfather looked out the window again. "Where the fuck are they? My flight plan says we're taking off in ten minutes. If they're not here in…."

"They'll be here."

Four minutes later, Raymond, Diondre and Rebecca pulled up in the limo. They jumped out of the car and ran for the plane.

When Raymond saw John Henry, his eyes turned to fire.

"I'm not going anywhere with this fucker."

With only minutes to spare, Sheba tried to stay calm. "He saved our lives, Raymond. Mercs bust in on us at The Godfather's condo. John Henry got us out in the nick of time."

"How convenient."

When John Henry saw his son, his face flushed with anger. They hadn't talked since the big fight at John Henry's house.

Diondre ignored his dad and his mother and found a seat in the back of the plane.

The Godfather shot Diondre a look that said don't disrespect your parents.

Diondre nodded at his father, then his mother. "Hey dad. Hey mom."

John Henry nodded a curt greeting. Sheba didn't respond but inside she was relieved beyond words to know he was alright.

Sheba swallowed her pride and asked Dee-dee about his pregnant girlfriend.

"Does Rebecca need anything? Some water maybe? A little Orange Juice?"

Rebecca was grateful. "Yes Mam. Some juice would be good. I feel a kind of dizzy."

A flight attendant magically appeared with a glass of ice, fresh squeezed OJ and a bag of pretzels.

The pilot's voice chimed in over the PA telling them to prepare for take-off. Seven soon to be fugitives strapped themselves in as the plane rolled onto the tarmac and ascended to an unknown destiny.

Sheba reached over the seat and tapped The Godfather on the shoulder. "I forgot to ask. Where are we going?"

"I'll let you know when we get there. I've got to go make a few calls. See you in a few hours," The Godfather said before walking up a flight of stairs to a private area of the plane.

Thirty-five

At Sheba's house, it didn't take the Mercs long to figure out the place was empty. The packed up and headed over to Beverly Hills. Six Mercs walked around The Godfather's empty apartment looking in closets, under beds and searching for a panic room. Half hour or so later, they linked up in the living room to communicate their frustration over the target's escape.

A man in a suede jacket said, "I visited all his main chill spots. Took out four of his best men. He's nowhere to be found and nobody's talking."

A man wearing a bullet proof vest with pockets stuffed with ammunition, knives and guns said, "I tortured his barber and even cut off one of his fingers—I'm pretty sure he has no idea where The Godfather is."

A third man with cold, dead eyes wearing a steel blue custom made suit said, "The man is a professional. He's been in the organization for two decades. He knows what to do. He's made himself invisible and taken the people he loves with him. I expect The Order to rescind the contract in the next few days. If I were you, I'd back off."

Without another word, the men nodded at each other respectfully, rose from their seats and parted ways.

*****

In another world, Violet Brown, the psychic, was asleep in bed and having a horrific nightmare. There was gunfire. People were running amuck. There was a teenaged boy with bright brown eyes hiding behind a table. A big burly man drove up in a Jeep. The woman Violet had done a reading for was crouched on the ground crying. An older man who looked like he could be her father was standing in front her. His body was riddled with bullets. Sheba screamed as her father went down amidst smoke and explosions. Sheba's shriek shook Violet out of the ghastly nightmare.

Violet bolted up to a sitting position in bed. Her body was covered with sweat and her breathing was erratic. Her mind centered in on finding Sheba and telling her she was in danger.

She dialed the number on the business card the woman had given her. Her call went straight to voicemail. She looked at the business name on the card. *Ransome Industries*. She had driven by those swanky offices before.

Violet jumped in her car and drove along PCH until she saw the building with the name of the company etched on the front. She walked up to the entrance and tried the door. It was locked. She stood back and look in the windows that weren't frosted.

It didn't take long for her to figure out that the building was empty. She sent Sheba a text asking her to call as soon as possible.

Violet got another message for Sheba as she pushed the send button. Sheba's life wasn't the only one in danger. She now had an unborn child to protect...

Violet was in the kitchen making herself a cup of tea when the phone rang. The man on the other end of the phone said he was Sheba's father. He said that his security detail had followed Sheba to her store and then he did an investigation on her.

Violet was a little taken back by his invasion of her privacy. But the man, who called himself The Godfather, said it was for his daughter's protection. Then the man also told her that he needed her to come to an undisclosed place to help his daughter and grandson get through a tough time. She was about to tell him how crazy he was and how she didn't even know if he was who he said he was when he told her about his contribution to a fund to help girls in Africa.

"I understand you are part of an organization that helps victims of human trafficking? Well, I'm prepared to make a sizeable donation to support that work. Would two-hundred and fifty thousand help get things going with your program?"

Violet had been speechless. When she got her voice back she told him, "Where do I catch the plane and what time do I need to be ready for your driver to pick me up?"

Thirty-six

Sheba could see nothing but crystal blue water over colorful reefs for miles and miles. That was the view out of the passenger window of The Godfather's private plane. Sheba felt them slowly making their descent into a mystery paradise after what seemed like hours in the air.

Sheba leaned forward and whispered in his ear for the second time during their flight. "It'd be great if we knew where you are taking us."

The Godfather chuckled. "You remind me so much of your mother. I ever tell you that?"

"That's wonderful. But it still doesn't tell me where we're going."

The Godfather stood up and clapped his hands three times. Everybody sat up and paid attention.

"After the plane lands, we're going to a safehouse. The safehouse is a place off grid, purchased in the name of a total stranger. In lieu of the secret nature of our location, I'll need everybody's cell phone. My tech guy is gonna scramble your signal to make your location appear to be where you were two hours ago."

One by one, everybody dropped their phones into a small black bag.

"It's important that nobody makes any calls to anybody you know. The Order will be tracking you because of your association with me. Don't worry, it'll all be over soon. I'm gonna call headquarters in a couple of hours and get this mess straightened out."

They landed on a small airstrip in the middle of nowhere between majestic mountains and two stunning waterfalls. A luxury bus loaded them up upon arrival. Scantily clad women blindfolded them as they were whisked off to yet another unknown destination.

"It's for your own safety," The Godfather told them as the bus pulled off.

A click on the clock later, the blindfolds were removed. This time the almost naked women greeted them with chilled Mimosas and placed aromatic Lei's around their neck.

The Godfather bid them all goodbye like he was the President of Wakanda. "I will meet you in two hours for dinner in the main lodge. Please enjoy my island to the fullest."

One by one, the women greeted them with the same sentence.

"Welcome to Indigo Island. Don't hesitate to ask for anything your heart desires. I will show you to your villa now."

As they made their way to the assigned villa, a question popped into Sheba's mind. She tapped John Henry on the shoulder.

"How did you know we were in trouble? The Godfather and I? How'd you know we needed help?"

"I'll tell you later. Right now, I need the three S's. Shit, shower, sleep."

The compound looked like something out of a tropical fantasy. The villas were built over the water and had state of the art everything. Sheba and Raymond headed straight for the shower to wash off a long and tumultuous day. They washed each other's back and let the water cascade over their heads and bodies until the stress started to fade away.

There were new clothes and shoes in their sizes hanging up in the closet. Sheba wondered how in the hell The Godfather had orchestrated that while they were thirty-thousand feet in the sky.

A few hours later, the Goddesses—that's what Sheba had started calling them—materialized to escort them to the main lodge for a late dinner. Dinner was a fabulous spread that tasted as good as it looked.

There was baked lobster, teriyaki salmon, duck confit, grilled veggies and sweet coconut rice. To drink they were served an amazing homemade mango iced tea and later gourmet coffee with New York Cheesecake for dessert. After everybody was fed and full, The Godfather stood to make another announcement.

"I wanted everyone to know that the bounty on my head has been removed. There was a modest fee to clear things up but the bill is settled. You can all relax and enjoy the island. I'll have my assistant bring you your phones."

Sheba didn't believe it could be that simple. "How can you be sure? What if they're just telling you that so they can find out where we are?"

"The agreement was a two-way deal. If anything happens to me, the repercussions on the other side of the fence will be equally damaging. Nobody wants that."

Sheba dared not ask what the *equally damaging repercussions* were. Obviously, The Godfather had something on The Order that would be devastating if acted on.

"Can you tell us where we are now?"

"A little island in the Bahamas between Half Moon Cay and Atlantis. I purchased the land when it was just a heap of sand and swaying palm trees. We named it Indigo after my Mother who was taken from her home in Africa."

Sheba was moved by that powerful piece of her history. She knew little about her Father's side of the family and every tidbit she learned felt like priceless pearls.

"Was that her name? Indigo?"

"Her name was Beulah. On the plantation they called her Blue. They said she had blue eyes like the men who raped and impregnated her."

"Do you have a picture of her?"

"There are a few rare photos of Madam Blue."

Diondre inserted himself in the conversation. "Madam Blue—she was my great grandmother?"

"That would be correct." The Godfather told him matter-of-factly.

The group went back to eating, drinking and socializing. Raymond put his arm around Sheba's shoulder and gently pulled her to him. He knew she was catching feelings about the story of Indigo.

"You okay?"

"I'm good. Wondering why they called her Madam."

"Why don't you ask him?"

"Not sure I want to know. My mother was a madam but not the kind you want to tell people about."

"I can understand you not wanting to know."

Raymond paused like he was contemplating asking her something then went for it. "Something else has been on my mind. The way you said John Henry just showed up to your father's apartment. I mean, you didn't call him right?"

"No, I didn't. I was wondering the same thing."

They eased over to where John Henry and his bomb shell were sitting. Sheba sat down next to him and Raymond sat down next to her.

"You finished eating?"

"Yeah, what's up?"

"You never did answer my question. How'd you know The Godfather and I were in trouble."

"Sheba, I've known your father for years. He was partly responsible for me getting in the game."

"What? Did you know he was my father?"

"Not at first. When I first started working for him I---"

"—When did you work for my father?!!!!"

"Hold on a minute. I'm trying to explain. I worked for him when I was a kid. Then the leaders changed and I was put under somebody else. I do remember visiting your Mother's house with him but I had no idea who she was or who you were when I met you ten years later. Then I heard a story about his ex-woman—your mama—on the streets. I put two and two together. Realized his Mamadee was your Dorothy Ransome."

Sheba shot up out of her seat. "What the fuck?! Why didn't you tell me he was my father!"

The banter in the dining room dropped to a low hush. Every eye turned their way to see how the next few minutes would play out.

"All these years—I thought he was dead. And you knew he was alive and living just a few miles from us. And you have the nerve to judge me! Fuck you, John Henry. Fuck you and the horse you rode in on."

232

John Henry stood up. "You better check yourself, She. I was honoring a promise I made and that was important too."

"More important than the promise you made to your son's mother? To the woman you said you loved and were married to?"

"I never lied to you. I just didn't tell you what I knew."

Raymond took her hand. "Calm down, Sheba."

Diondre came over to the table and stood behind his mother. Then The Godfather walked over to where they were sitting.

"Sheba, he did it for your protection. I told him you and Diondre might not be safe if people found out I was your father."

"Well, somebody should've let me decide whether knowing my father was worth the risk."

"Sheba, The Order might've come after you and then I...."

Sheba was crying. "I needed a father! I needed a man to teach me how to love a man and how to be loved *by* a man. Mama taught me the game. She taught me how to shield my heart and get paper. But she never taught me how to give myself to another human being. How to allow them to love me and trust the way squares do it."

The Godfather tapped her on the shoulder. She spun around to face him.

Without looking away from her he said, "Everybody except Diondre, Raymond and John Henry, please leave the room."

The Goddesses exited the lodge along with John Henry's bombshell and Rebecca.

When they were gone, The Godfather said, "Come to me my daughter. Come here."

She took one step toward him.

"I want you to lay your head on my shoulder. Let me give you a little of the love I've held for you all these years."

She took two more steps toward him.

He took two steps toward her.

She laid her head on his left shoulder. Smelled his brisk cologne. Nestled her cheek into his manly contours.

"I thought I was all alone here. Mama was gone, you were gone—I had no kin I could turn to. It was hard."

He embraced her. Patted her a few times like he was comforting a baby. Sheba wailed the cry of a little girl who felt safe for the first time in her life.

The Godfather broke another one of his life rules. He apologized.

"I never should've left you. I'm sorry. I'll never leave you again."

The Godfather looked over at Diondre.
"Come to me, grandson."

Diondre went to his right shoulder. The Godfather embraced him and told him, "I want you to know I forgive you. You were being a man and protecting what was yours. That's what an honorable man is supposed to do."

"I'm sorry Godfather—I mean *Grandfather.* I thought you were trying to…"

"That's over and done. Let's never talk about it again."

The Godfather turned Sheba's shoulders toward him and lifted her chin until her eyes were facing his. "I took the liberty of paying off all your debts. You're free now. You can have a better life than I and your mother had. You don't have to look over your shoulder anymore or worry about the authorities knocking on your door."

"You did what? I owed my clients nearly a half million dollars."

"Don't worry about it. It's done."

Raymond stepped up. "I'm putting our house up for sale. We need a new start. And I need to do what I should've done long ago."

"What are you talking about Ray?"

Raymond dropped down on one knee. "Sheba, it would make me the happiest man on the planet if you would be my wife."

Sheba started crying again. Her tears segued into laughter.

"You know I'm a handful right? I'm spoiled. Selfish. Self-centered. Moody. Emotional as hell. You gonna stop me?"

"Hell no. You're telling the truth."

They all cracked up on that. Everybody except for John Henry.

The Godfather called him out. "John Henry. You were just a youngin' when they brought you into this game. You've been like a son to me. You see where this life leads you right? If you want out, I can make that happen."

"This life….this is all I know. Don't know what else an old Kingpin can do."

"Let's talk about that when we get back. But for now, I'm going need you to start respecting Raymond as the head of your son's mother's household. And it's time for you to start being a real father to your son."

John Henry was quiet for a minute. Then he stepped into the circle and spoke his piece.

"Sheba, I didn't know what I had when God gave me you. I was a broken man. Still am. Only thing I ever learned from my daddy was how to gamble, con and swindle people and mistreat women. My daddy sold me to The Order and I became their slave before I even knew what being a man was all about. I apologize for everything I did and everything I didn't do."

Sheba's face was on fire with tears. She couldn't talk. All she could do was listen to the words she had waited years to hear.

John Henry continued. "Dee-dee, I know I failed you again and again. As a father and as a man I gave you the best I had. Unfortunately, that wasn't very much."

John Henry fought the tears back like a warrior. "I thank the Lord above that Raymond stepped up and gave you what you needed to be better than me. And I know with him marrying your mama, you have a chance at a life that I never did."

Diondre walked over to his father and threw his arms around him.

"I love you, dad."

John Henry froze when he son said that. Raymond walked over to them and picked up John Henry's hand and wrapped it around his son's shoulder.

John Henry nodded his respect to Raymond who went back and stood by Sheba.

Then John Henry said three words to his son. Three words he'd never heard his father say.

"I love you, son. Everything is gonna be alright. We're gonna get through this."

Sheba turned around to face Raymond.

"The answer is yes. I will marry you. I will be your wife. I will be faithful to you. I will trust you with my heart. I will give you all of me. I will do my best to honor and respect you. I will build with you. I will not run away when I get scared even though I might want to."

Raymond kissed the back of her hand. "That's all I need. I got the rest."

The Godfather took over again.

"Well, this is about all the emotional shit I can handle." They all cracked up.

"We have a few days to rest up on the island. Massages, facials, swimming with the dolphins, eating organic food grown by my staff. Then it's time to go home and resurrect Ransome Industries."

Diondre stepped up. "Hold on a minute. Yall are forgetting something. I didn't get to speak."

John Henry extended his hand toward the center spot and called his seed forward.

"Let the youngblood have his say."

238

Diondre walked into the circle. "Three things. One—we've been through a lot. I know its gonna make us stronger. I mean, we already strong--but this took our bond to the next level. You guys taught me a lot with your mistakes. And I learned a few lessons of my own along the way. As you know, I'm gonna be a father. I need to finish college so my kid will have a future and...I'mah need a lot of help."

Sheba spoke up. "You got it, son. I'm here for you. We're all here for you."

Everybody nodded in agreement.

Diondre continued. "Two—I want to start some kind of program for kids who want to get out of the drug game. I'm naming it the Kite Flight Program after my friend, Kite, who was killed in a drug bust."

Raymond walked over and did a fist bump, Black power handshake with Diondre.

"That's real good, man. I know a few people who might fund your program. Let's talk business after we get back to the mainland."

The Godfather nodded his approval. He mind was already churning with ideas to help Diondre launch his dream.

"Last thing. Number three. I want Ronnie to be my daughter's Godmother. She's been there for me my whole life. She was the one who taught me how to play ball. She was there for my moms when the bottom dropped out."

The Godfather stepped into the circle again.

"I was waiting for the right time to announce this. Several guests have joined us since we've been on the island. They're very tired from the flight and are resting in their cottages. They will meet us here in the morning for a final conversation."

Sheba interjected. "You gonna drop that on us and then make us wait until the morning to find out who they are."

The Godfather chuckled. "You are so much like your mother."

He clapped his hands twice like he was talking to a group of children.

"I'm turning in. We have a big day tomorrow. Our flight takes off at 10:46am. Breakfast is at eight. Don't be late. Bonne nuit. Good night, everyone."

Thirty-seven

Around eight a.m. bodies began to emerge from their cubby holes and drift toward the main lodge. Sheba and Raymond made their way down the path. Three limos were parked in front of the lodge. It didn't take long for her to figure out that whoever had arrived had already exited and was waiting inside. Her and Raymond climbed the steps hand in hand, both in their own thoughts and not knowing what or who they would face when they opened the door.

Diondre and Rebecca were inside sitting down. Sheba turned to see John Henry and his Latin Bombshell coming down the path toward the lodge. The Goddesses were flitting around the dining room setting out breakfast and doing what they did best. The Godfather hadn't arrived yet.

The Godfather had cordoned off a section of the main lodge. There were four curtains hanging side by side and Sheba could just make out the outer edges of chairs that sat behind the curtains. Sheba had a feeling that whatever was about to be revealed would change her life forever.

The group did their best to eat some of the delicious breakfast the Goddesses had put out. But curiosity took precedence over hunger. When The Godfather entered the space, they all stopped eating and turned around to witness the big unveiling.

"Good morning everyone. I hope you slept well and woke feeling replenished. Today is a very important day. Today we reenter the world we left behind. We aren't going back to our old lives. We're starting over with brand new

241

rules and obligations. And it is the old life that we shall kill and bury before we leave Indigo Island."

He paused to take a sip of the champagne the Goddess Amina had placed in his hand.

"As some of you know, over the years I had to make some hard decisions to keep my family safe. I had to investigate and track anyone who came into my daughter's or my grandson's life. I also had to put people in place who could keep an eye on you. Today, you will meet some of those people and be reunited with people I had to hide so that you and them could remain safe."

Sheba's heart started pounding. It took everything she had not to jump up, run over to the curtains and snatch them back.

The Godfather walked over the first curtain and put his hand on a satin rope.

"Behind this curtain is someone I put in place to keep Sheba and my grandson Diondre safe. I apologize for invading your privacy but I couldn't take a chance on something happening to you."

He slid back the curtain and to Sheba's shock sat the Rawmeister, her personal chef and butler.

Diondre jumped out of his seat and shouted, "The Rawmeister!!!! What the fu...I mean, what the heck? You work for my Grandfather? Dangggggg. That's crazy."

Sheba shook her head back and forth. "Every phone conversation. Every guest that came to our home. The Godfather knew about it through you. And you knew all this time that my father was alive and well."

The Rawmeister nodded his head in agreement. "I never meant to hurt you or Diondre. The Godfather works for some unscrupulous people—people that we couldn't let know he had a daughter and a grandson that could be targeted."

Sheba had called on her Alpha Wolf to deal with the betrayal. It was the Alpha that kept her calm in situations where she wanted to tear the head off someone who lied to her.

"I understand. I'm not even mad. It wasn't personal, it was business. I'm good. Let's keep it pushing. What's behind curtain number two?"

"I'm getting to that. But first, I want to announce that the Rawmeister and his family are leaving the country and moving to an undisclosed location for a few months. I want to thank him for his excellent service and keeping my family safe."

Sheba chimed in, "Wait a minute. How am I gonna make it without the Rawmeister's green juice, cheese grits and salmon patties with avocado salsa?"

The Rawmeister cracked up at that. "I have a book coming out which is dedicated to you, Diondre and Raymond. It has all my recipes in it."

Sheba walked over and hugged his neck. Diondre and Raymond did a soul hand shake with him and quietly went back to their seats.

The Godfather prepared to raise the next curtain.
"This next person is an old friend. I had nothing to do with her and you coming together Sheba but once she realized who you were, she called me. She used to service your Mother when she was alive."

"What do you mean by *service*?"

"She did work for her. She read the cards, the leaves and the shells to keep the wolves from killing my Dorothy when she was out doing business."

"So whoever is behind the next curtain is a she. Okay. Let's get on with it. I feel like I'm about to have a panic attack over here."

He pulled back curtain number two and behind the curtain was the psychic, Violet Brown.

Sheba shot up and out of her chair. "Get the fuck out of here. You know the psychic lady? Is that how she knew so much about what was going on in my life?"

John Henry chimed in. "I remember Mamadee talking about a psychic she worked with."

The Godfather set the record straight. "I never told her anything about you. Violet works with people across the world. Her psychic abilities once saved the lives of two hundred African girls who'd been kidnapped by human

244

traffickers. When you did the reading with her she put two and two together and called me to see if they were four."

"How did she know my Mama?"

Violet stood up. "If I may answer, Godfather?"

The Godfather nodded his approval.

"Dorothy Ransome and I met many years ago when she was starting her business. She'd been having dreams of a little girl dressed in wolf's clothing and couldn't make sense of it. I did a reading for her and told her that the wolf was her totem animal. I also told her that the little girl in her dreams was her daughter. She laughed at that because at the time, you hadn't been born yet. And she wasn't planning on having kids."

"So you knew my mother before you knew The Godfather?"

"That's correct."
"Go on."

"I did rituals in my tradition to keep your mother safe and to bring wealth. I'm not allowed to do negative work for anyone so that was how I served her. I also told her she was sick and that she needed to get her affairs in order. I knew she didn't have long."

Sheba felt the tears building up between her eyelids. She choked them back and regained her composure.

"Did you know who I was when you did the reading for me?"

245

"You looked familiar but it had been so long since I'd seen you that I wasn't sure. But after we did the reading I started to get messages from your Mother."

"Messages? What....what did she say?"

"She said to tell you she's sorry. She did her best to raise you but knows she made a lot of mistakes."

"She did good. Damn good. She kept me safe. We lived in a beautiful house in a good neighborhood. I wore designer clothes, went to private schools and had the best of everything."

"She says her biggest mistake was not teaching you how to love unconditionally."

"Is she talking to you right now?"

"Yes. She is here. She is very happy that her family is together and that you are finally healing."

"Can I ask her something." Sheba said in a voice so small and innocent it was almost a whisper.

"Sure. I may not get an answer but ask away."

"Did she love me? Was she really going to send me to live with her sister?"

"She says of course she loved and still loves you. And she never would've sent you anywhere."

Sheba let the tears fall.

"Tell her I love her and miss her too."

Violet whispered something under her breath.

Sheba strained to hear her. "Huh? What'd you say?"

"I was telling her what you said."

"Okay, this is getting a little too deep."

Diondre stepped up. "Can I ask Grandma something?"

Violet started laughing.

"What's funny?"

"She said, don't call her grandma. She ain't nobody's damn grandma. She is the Grand Mother."

Sheba cracked up. "That's my mama. I wasn't totally sure this was real but that sealed it."

"What's your question young man. We have to hurry because the door is closing."

"Am I having a boy or a girl?"

"You sure you want to know?"

Diondre and Rebecca nodded yes.

"It's a girl."

Rebecca threw her arms around Diondre. "Yes! I knew it!"

"That's cool. A daughter. Thanks."

John Henry said, "I'm gonna be a grandfather. Damn. Yall making me feel old."

The Godfather stepped up. "Congratulations Diondre and Rebecca. Unfortunately, that's all the time we have to partake in Violet's amazing gift.
But she will be supporting Sheba throughout this transition and beyond. She will also be helping Diondre and Rebecca with the baby."

Sheba nodded her head gratefully. "I'd like that."

Sheba turned her attention to the third curtain. "Who is behind the curtain? I can't think of anyone else that might've infiltrated my life to spy on me and my son."

The Godfather summoned Sheba over to the curtain.

"Why don't you open this one."

"I can't. I'm too nervous. I can hardly breathe as it is."

Raymond put his arm around her shoulder. "It's okay, Baby. Take a deep breath."

Raymond massaged her shoulders and the back of her neck like he always did when she was overwhelmed.

John Henry stood up.

"I'll open the curtain."

The Godfather nodded. "Actually, that's quite appropriate."

John Henry walked over to the curtain and put his hand on the rope.

The Godfather put his hand over John Henry's hand.

"Before you open this curtain I need to tell you something. We've been following someone that your father knew. The Order makes it their business to track family members of their employees. When your father died, they stopped following this person. But I continued to keep a man on her just in case."

"Who is she?"

"She—Vanessa Henry is your sister. Your half-sister. Your father had another family in Las Vegas."

"What the hell you talking about?"

"Open the curtain and meet your sister."

John Henry snatched the curtain back.

There were two people sitting behind the curtain. The woman stood up and opened her arms. She looked just like his father.

"Hello John Henry. I'm your sister, Vanessa."

John Henry was speechless.

"I have a sister?"

The two of them hugged, laughed and both of them cried.

"I have a sister, yall! I thought it was just me out here. I got kinfolk!" John Henry said picking her up and spinning her around.

Diondre walked up and around his father to the other person sitting behind the curtain.

"There's someone else back here. A curtain behind the curtain. Can I lift this one?"
The Godfather nodded, "Sure, son. Go right ahead."

Diondre pulled the rope slowly to reveal the fourth guest.

"Fabian! Man, what you doing here?"

Sheba walked over and stood next to Diondre.

Sheba asked, "Father, why is this trash here?"

"Because he came to you for help and the help you gave him wasn't the help he needed. And because everybody deserves a second chance. You, of all people, should agree with that. Diondre didn't get a chance to help his friend Kite. But maybe he can help his other friend."

Fabian stood up in front of her and spread his arms wide.

"I'm sorry, Mama Ransome. I was stupid. Out there showing off trying to act like I was something I'm not. There was something I didn't tell you when you interviewed me. I didn't tell you because I didn't know what I was."

"My name is Fabian and I'm an addict. Please forgive me. Y'all are all I got. My mama died yesterday."

Diondre walked over and hugged his homeboy.

The Godfather waited a few minutes and shared his plan.

"Fabian is going into a rehab when he leaves here. If he gets clean, I will be paying for his college education. I've already got him an apartment. He'll be right up the street from Diondre and Rebecca."

Sheba was quiet for a few minutes then she spoke up. "I guess you're right. Everybody deserves a second chance. I thank God that I'm getting one."

She opened her arms and received Fabian.

"I'm glad you're getting help."

After the curtain game was finished, they pulled the tables together and ate and laughed and talked. One big happy family. The Latin Bombshell even spoke up.

251

"I thought John Heenry was going to get me killed. I thought he was loco. Instead he gave me life. I had no idea when I told him what I heard at the party that I would be here to see this beautiful family come together. Or that the threat of death would bring life to so many."

John Henry kissed her on the lips. "Daddy got something for you later on."

"Si, mi amor." She answered batting her eyes seductively.

Just then the door to the lodge opened and another life changer entered the room.

The group turned around to face her. She had a pretty blonde lady on her arm.

Diondre jumped up out of his seat. "Ronnie! Aw snap, what's up Big Ro!"

"What's up, Godson. Sorry I'm late. I was with a client and couldn't get away."

The Godfather stood to welcome her. "Welcome, Veronica. You're the last to arrive to our little family party. And welcome to your friend, Sable."

Ronnie's girlfriend nodded a curt greeting to everyone.

"Thank you for inviting me—for inviting us—to be a part of this day. In case yall didn't know, The Godfather had the whole event live streamed on his private plane so us latecomers could be a part of it."

Sheba shook her head back and forth. "Of course he did. Is there anything you can't do?" She walked over and hugged Ronnie and gave her a kiss on the cheek.

One by one, everybody came over and greeted Ronnie and her partner, made them feel a part of the energy of their incredible morning.

An hour later, the group boarded two separate planes. The Godfather's plane had Violet, Sheba, Raymond, Diondre and Rebecca. The other plane had John Henry, his Latin Bombshell as well as Ronnie, Ronnie's Partner, Fabian, the Rawmeister and John Henry's sister. The Godfather had separated them to throw off anybody who might be tracking them.

The Godfather's plane set down at LAX in the area where charter planes came in. As he moved through customs he took note of a superbly dressed Black man who watched their every move.

After their passports were stamped and they were officially back on American soil, the detective walked over to where they were picking up their luggage.

He flashed a badge and identification card that had the numbers 3333 and the name Detective Zion Justice underneath.

"Simon Wellington the third. It's a pleasure to finally meet you, Sir. That was a real slick move booking two planes. Intuition led me to the right door."

Sheba had never known her father's real name until that moment. The Godfather walked a few yards away from the group. Sheba followed them. The detective continued grilling him.

"I hear you're getting out of the game. That's cool and all but you left a lot of blood on these streets. That blood will one day lead to a trail for us to uncover all the dirt you did. And you will pay for those crimes. I'll see to it."

The Godfather's voice was as calm as a morgue at six a.m. when he answered. "I appreciate your sincerity. But that bill has already been paid in full."

"You could never completely pay a bill that big. Not as long as you're alive."

"So you're the judge and the jury? God decides the debt His children are to pay not man."

"You wanna talk to me about God? You think you *are* God."

"You're mistaken kind sir. It's true. I'm one of God's fallen angels. But that doesn't matter now. What you need to understand is this: death can't kill me. Justice takes on the form that we give it. I've paid a steep price for my sins. More than you can comprehend."

"Your philosophizing doesn't impress me. I'm a logical man. An eye for an eye."

Sheba was the next one he talked to.

"And you, mam, are free because we didn't catch you with your hand in the cookie jar. But that doesn't mean you're innocent. The Gods are giving you a second chance but there won't be a third. Step wrong and I'll pounce on you like a lion pounces on his prey."

Sheba nodded at him and said, "Where I come from, the lions and wolves respect each other's territory. They don't put their paws on my cubs and I continue to let their children roam free."

"Are you threatening my family?"

Sheba didn't answer.

"Just so we're clear, I'm not here to kill the wolves. I'm here to protect the sheep that the wolves want to devour."

"All the sheep have been freed, detective. You must've missed that memo."

"Yeah, I must've missed it. I'll check my *files* when I get back to the office."

Sheba knew he mentioned files because The Godfather's scrambling of the encryption codes had prevented them from downloading Sheba's financial records.

"And tell that ex-Kingpin of yours, John Henry, I'm checking for him too. He better keep his nose clean. One slip and I'm taking him down."

"I heard John Henry was retired. He's probably somewhere toking Cuban cigars, dunking coins in dollar slots and playing house with one of his girlfriends."

Detective Justice nodded his understanding and turned his attention to Diondre who has just walked up.

"Young blood, if you ever want to talk again, you know where to find me."

Sheba stepped in front of him. "Like I said, keep your paws off my cubs, Detective."

Sheba's eyes had fire in them. The wolf in her was always prepared to do anything to keep her seed safe. Detective Justice backed off.

Diondre took Rebecca's hand in his and said, "I ain't got nothing for you, Detective. Our business is done."

"Well, remember, God is always watching. Even when we think we're hiding something from Him. God sees all."

The Godfather stepped up. "I think you've said enough. Tata detective. See you around."

With that, Detective Zion Justice tipped his hat and strolled off.

There would be other wars to fight but their battle with Justice was done for now.

*****

Three months later, Sheba and Raymond got married at sea on a luxurious yacht. Violet performed the ceremony. Everybody from Indigo Island was present and accounted for at their nuptials. Violet was her Matron of honor. Ronnie was her Maid of Honor. The Godfather lovingly walked her down the aisle into the arms of Raymond. John Henry not only showed up but acted like he had some sense.

After the wedding was over, John Henry had a few words to say to Sheba.

"I'm happy for you and Ray. I mean that."

"Thanks. I appreciate that."

"But there's only one John Henry. And if that negro ever steps out of line…."

Raymond walked up behind them. "You don't have to worry about that, man. My wife will always be treated like the queen she is."

The bulls shook hands and went to their mutual corners. Sheba exhaled.

Six months later, Diondre graduated from college and got drafted to the NBA to play for the Lakers. He also became the father of a six pound, ten-ounce baby girl who they named, Indigo. Sheba and the tribe spoiled the hell out of Indigo. Sheba loved being a grandmother and spent a lot of her free time bonding with her new granddaughter.

One morning, Diondre called Sheba and asked her to take a ride with him. She let her team know she'd be late and

met her son at a local Starbuck's. She got in the car with him
and they rode a few miles to a blue building in West
Hollywood. The sign outside said, "Indigo Center."

"What is this place, son?"

"It's a surprise. Come inside, ma. I want you to see
something."

The inside of the building looked like an upscale
hospital. They passed by rooms with beds inside. Sheba saw
men and women in the rooms. Some were sleeping. Others
were nervously pacing the floor. Nurses in bright blue scrubs
hovered over them giving them medicine and care.

Diondre took Sheba's hand as they entered two double
doors. Behind the double doors was a large room with baby
beds. There were about a dozen babies being cared for by
nurses. Some of the babies appeared to be very ill. A few had
tubes in their tiny bodies.

"What's wrong with the babies, son?"

"Their mothers were addicted to crack when they were
pregnant with them."

"Oh my God."

Sheba zeroed in on one little baby girl who had a pink
bow in her hair. "Why is her hand shaking like that?"

"That's what cocaine does to the body of an embryo."

"This is….this is what I caused."

"That's the past. Indigo is the future. Indigo is going to help the Mothers and the babies get better. And the fathers too. Indigo is my drug treatment and recovery center. Raymond and The Godfather raised the money to launch the facility last month."

"I'm....I'm proud of you."

"One more thing. There's somebody I want you to see."

They walked down a long hall, back through the double doors, back to the adult side of the building. Diondre turned right and went to room number five. Sheba saw a young Black man sitting on the bed. When he turned around, Sheba realized it was Fabian.

Diondre said, "What up, man? How you doing today?"

Fabian stood up and hugged his homeboy.

"Ain't no thing but a chicken wing my brother."

Sheba nodded at him. "You look good, Fabian. Like new money."

"Thanks to your big head son I have four months clean. I got me a sponsor and everything. I'm leaving Indigo today and start college tomorrow."

"I'm proud of you, Godson."

"I'm your Godson again?"

"You heard me, right?"

"Thanks Mama Ransome!" He came over and hugged her tight.

"When you graduate from college, they'll be a job waiting for you at Ransome Industries."

"Thanks! I'mah take you up on that."

Diondre took her hand and they headed back to the car.

"I have one more place I want to take you."

On the ride to wherever they were going, Sheba processed what she'd just seen.

"Never, ever again will I be a part of babies ending up like that. Or their mamas and daddies."

"Me either. I don't want drug money to pay for nothing in my life."

"So where we going now, son?"

"We're here. Come inside with me."

Sheba thought they were at another medical facility. But once they got inside, Sheba realized it was something different.

"Is this is marijuana dispensary?"

"Yep. My grandfather invested in five of these bad boys. And they are raking in the dough."

"Thought he was out of the drug business."

"Marijuana is legal, mom. Don't you keep up with the news?"

"I guess you're right, son."

They walked into a back section of the store. Diondre was buzzed into a smaller area off to the side. When they went in the room Sheba saw him. He was sitting behind a desk with multiple camera screens. The one and only John Henry.

For the first time in his life, John Henry had a straight job. He was head of security for The Godfather's new company, *Nature's Pharmaceuticals*, which turned marijuana into medicine.

"What's up old man?"

"Still getting paper and being a boss."

"Your son took me to see his new place of business."

"I checked it out last week."

Sheba was shocked John Henry had visited Indigo before her. She let a streak of jealousy go by and focused on the present.

"So, why are we here, son?"

"Me and Rebecca are getting married. I wanted to tell you together. The wedding will take place at Indigo Island. We're going to Christen the baby while we're there."

"That's real good, son. Let me know the dates so I can block my calendar."

John Henry stood up and man-hugged his son. "Proud of you, G. That's some real man shit right there."

"That's why you got us together? To tell us about the wedding?"

"No, I have some other news. I'm quitting ball. I want to be present for my daughter. B-ball requires me to travel constantly."

"That's been your dream for a long time. How you feel about that?"

"Like it's the right thing to do."

John Henry spoke up. "I've seen firsthand what it's like to be away from your kid when they're growing up. You miss all kinds of important stuff. But I also know what it's like to wake up and realize it's too late to go for your dreams. Maybe there's a way you can do both. Will and Jada did it."

"They had millions of dollars. Nannies. Pilots. Chefs. That made it easy."

Sheba echoed John Henry's statements. "You might want to talk to your Grandfather and see what can be done to make sure you're present for those important moments.

Playing for the Lakers pays pretty well too if I'm not mistaken."

"Maybe I will. See, that's why I wanted to talk to my parents. Y'all old but you know a little something something."

They all cracked up at that.
John Henry stood up. Sheba quietly took in the dips and folds of his solid body. He was still fine as hell.

"I gotta get back to work. Thanks for stopping by. Let me know about the wedding."

They all hugged their goodbyes. Sheba felt John Henry's hands around her waist when they embraced.

"You take care, She. See you around."

Ronnie brought her new girlfriend Sable by the office so Sheba could get to know her. A few minutes into their convo, Sheba decided she liked Sable and that she really was good for Ronnie.

Sheba left work early to hear Raymond play the guitar with a small R&B band called the *Soul Circuit*. The guitar was Raymond's second love.
Raymond was happier than he had ever been in his entire life. Him and Sheba had the normal arguments married couples had but their love was strong and getting stronger every day. And their passion was like a fire that never died out.

Violet and Sheba bonded like glue. Violet was the Mother energy Sheba had always wanted and so desperately needed when she was growing up. Violet was the perfect combination of firm and loving to keep Sheba's wolf calm and peaceful.

Sheba found out that Violet and her father had started spending mornings at the beach meditating together. Sheba was happy about that. Her father needed softening up after years of being hard as stone.

Violet told Sheba about her husband passing away. Violet had been single ever since. She was glad to have a man to dote over.

One morning when Violet and Simon were sitting at the ocean, Violet told him he needed to exorcise his demons. In an effort to be obedient to her guidance, he booked a yacht to take them to the Cayman Islands. When the yacht was out in the middle of the ocean he jumped into the sea and asked the Water Gods to cleanse him of his darkness. The next day, Violet told him it worked. Soon, they were doing way more than meditating together...

Violet was visiting with Diondre, Rebecca and Indigo one morning when John Henry stopped by. She hadn't seen him since that day at the medicinal store.

After spending some time with the baby, he sat on the terrace with Sheba and together they lamented on how far they'd both come.

"If you would've told me we'd be living this life, I would've told you that you were crazy. I mean, I ain't totally square or nothing. I still have a few demons left in me. But I ain't doing nothing I could get time for."

Sheba cracked up. "Sometimes I do miss the crazy just a little. But I wouldn't change this world for nothing. Mama didn't have a chance at a life free of worry and paranoia. But me, I'm gonna enjoy the peace. Don't get it twisted, I'm gonna keep getting my paper but not at the expense of my safety or freedom."

"You ever wonder what would've happened if we stayed together? You know I would've kept you on your toes and you never would've gotten bored, not for a second."

"You're about to mess up a perfect moment, old man."

"Old? Look at these abs and these arms."

"Yeah, you still look good. You alright."

"And I'm still John Henry. Real freaks don't die we just do our freakiness in secret."

"That's TMI. To answer your question, yes, I have thought about what would've happened if we stayed together. And yeah, I probably would've never been bored. But being bored every now and then is okay. It's also a sign that things are really good. I'm clear that our reason for coming together was that child in there and our granddaughter. We had some good times but that part of our relationship is done. All I want to do is stack my paper, travel and enjoy the blessings God has given me."

"I feel you on that. Auight, She. I'm out of here. Give Raymond my respect."

"I'll do that. Take good care, John Henry."

She watched him walk away. He seemed a little sad and she couldn't figure out why. After John Henry left, Diondre came in from working out.

"Hey mom. What's crack-a-lacking?"

"You got the best hand, son. About to bounce and go get packed for me and Ray's vacation."

"Where yall going this year?"

"It's a secret. We never tell anybody until we get back. I know it's crazy but it works for us."

"Do *you*, Mama. I do have some news for you though. I'm being recruited for the Knicks."

"Thought you wanted to stay close to home. You thinking about leaving your beloved Lakers? All your life you wanted to play for them. Since you were a little boy that's all you talked about."

"Wasn't it you that told me change is good?"

"Well, I've learned a few things since then. Change is good but so is stability. So is surety."

"Ain't nothing sure but three things. Life, death and I'm gonna stay Black and be successful."

"That's four things, son."

"I'm jes' saying. Life doesn't promise you anything. So, if an opportunity comes along you check it out. Just in case."

"I hear you, son. You do you."

He laughed and told her, "That's what I'm saying. Love you, Mama. Like a well-done New York steak with mash potatoes and gravy."

"Like Belgium waffles with honey butter, fresh strawberries and maple syrup."

"Like barbecue chicken, candied yams and collard greens."

They high-fived and Sheba told him, "You won, son! Now can we go get some lunch because you done made me hungry."

"Me too, Mama. My treat!"

Thirty-eight

Sheba and Raymond were in Greece on their annual Happy Couple's Honeymoon. Each year they selected a new exotic destination to keep their marriage exciting and unpredictable. Wrapped in huge white towels, they ventured down the path to an unoccupied area. They dipped their feet in the sun-warmed ocean that sparkled in a beautiful crystal blue under what looked like a painted sky.

On their private beach, Sheba laid a towel on the sand, poured Raymond a glass of champagne and dropped a few strawberries in the glass. Raymond laid his towel down next to the one Sheba put down for him and pulled the picnic basket within reach of their sexy party.

Raymond stretched out on his back and rested his head over his folded elbows. Sheba did the same as they let the hot sun cook and sooth them just a bit. The water cooled their feet as it lapped the shore.

"This is the life."

"It's a good life. A very good life."

"You ever miss all the excitement and drama you had with your ex?"

"Why you go there? Glad you didn't say his name though. Don't want to bring that energy to such a holy place. And no, I don't miss being scared for me and my son's life or knowing any day could be the end of my world. Now can we change the subject?"

After a few glasses of bubbly, Sheba shed her towel and eased her naked body down onto Raymond's lap. She rubbed her soft flesh against him until she woke the master. He pretended he didn't know what she was doing until the monster in him forced him to surrender a deep moan. Sheba picked up a bottle of dark liquid and poured it down her body. Chocolate liqueur melted down her skin from head to toe.

Sheba turned around and scooted up Raymond's body until her Yoni was over his mouth. She rode his face until he sucked every ounce of the chocolate from between her legs.

"Oh yes, baby. Just like that. Suck it. That's so good, Daddy."

Raymond sucked soft then hard. He pulled and kneaded her pearl with his lips. Then he gently locked her flesh between his teeth and used his tongue to massage it. His strong hands gripped her ass and pushed her body into his mouth again and again.

Sheba's nectar rolled down his chin onto his chest. He continued sucking, taking her almost to the point of exploding and backing up to build the pleasure.

"Suck this fucking pussy—oh my God—you are so fucking good."

Raymond dined on her pleasure until she couldn't take any more. She tried to back up off his tongue but he had her trapped. She was forced to feel the power of his tongue dancing against her womb.

"Oh shit, Ray…..I'm about to fucking come for you. Please…please make this pussy come for you!"

Sheba's spirit went out of her body as the orgasm ripped through her and made her scream a menagerie of obscenities.

"Please—oh my God. I'm coming so hard. Raymond-daddy-baby. Please don't stop. Keep fucking me! I'm still coming!"

When she came back to earth, Raymond flipped her over and pulled her ass high in the air. He slid into her slow. The juices from her climax drenched him and made him release an animalistic shriek of pleasure.

"Ahhhhh. You are so fucking wet baby."

Sheba's head was on the towel and her hands were on each side of her head keeping her body balanced. Raymond pulled out a few inches and slid into her again. Sheba slammed her ass toward him and squeezed her vaginal muscles around the shaft.

"Level three baby. Slow it down. Daddy wants to enjoy this."

Sheba slowed down but kept riding it steady. When she came off of him, she squeezed her muscles as hard as she could.

Raymond laughed a wicked laugh. "You…damn baby. You such a bad bitch. Yes, you are."

"Yes, I fucking am a bad bitch. Now give me what I want. Give me that dick. All of it! Don't hold back nothing!"

He pulled out of her. It damn near made him come but he held on for the perfect finish he wanted.

He turned her around and made her face him. He picked her up, positioned her Yoni on his member and entered her again. She held him around his shoulders and wrapped her legs around his back. He looked out at the ocean as she bounced up and down on him.

"Oh shit, Raymond. Your dick is rubbing against my clit....Fuck—take this pussy—this is your fucking pussy damnit! I'm gonna come again. Oh fuck! I'm gonna fucking come again. Come with me!"

He grabbed her ass, pushed her into him and rode her hard.

A few minutes later, they exploded like an atomic bomb.

Both of them were screaming, moaning and crying. Their pleasure was other worldly and ego didn't stand a chance.

After they calmed down, they swam out into the warm ocean water and cooled their flesh. Sheba embraced him and kissed him like she was searching for her purpose on his tongue.

"I love you, Raymond. You are my eternal. You are the one I want to grow old next to. Today I give you my heart and soul."

Raymond smiled and told her, "For so many years I prayed to love you this way and for you to trust me enough to love me back the same. I thank you for the gift of your vulnerability. I will guard it with my life."

"Look up at the sky, baby."

He looked up just in time to see a plane writing a message. It said, "Forever yours, eternally mine. ETL"

"You….what the hell am I going to do with you?"

"I don't know but you'll never get bored trying to figure it out."

"This life of ours is crazy but one thing it isn't and never has been, is boring."

"Well, I have a little opportunity I want to talk to you about."
"Is it legal?"

"Legal is the only game I play now. But it is a little dangerous."

"Danger is my middle name."

"Wanna play some more?"

"I thought you knew. I'll never get enough of you….

Thirty-nine

Paris, France.

The Godfather was there to expand his marijuana business to a global market. He'd chosen Paris for the launching point because France was his familiar. It was the place where his life began and in some ways, the place where his early life had ended abruptly.

Sheba had only known his persona. The Godfather. Her overseer. The ruthless Kingpin who got rich off of people's weaknesses. Like the Greek God, Thanatos, Simon regularly decided the date people ceased to exist. And even though the lives he took were primarily those who deserved to die, he knew that playing God was wrong no matter the reason.

Sheba had never known the man beneath the surface. He was the only man her mother had ever loved. A man who endured the pain of watching his daughter grow up from afar. Not being able to pinch her chubby cheeks when she laughed or comfort her when she cried. It had been an excruciating existence.

And then he became the great revealer. Unveiling the lies told by both her of parents. Lies by her chef, her children's father and a woman who'd become like a mother to her. The Godfather wondered if Sheba would ever be able to trust him.

She'd called him a few hours after they got back to Los Angeles with another shitload of questions. She'd researched his surname and found out they were descendants of the Monarch. She wanted to know the truth about who his parents were and most importantly, how and why the angel had fallen.

What he wondered was, after she learned the truth, would she still want a relationship with him? They'd bonded in the midst of a major crisis but now that the excitement was over, would Sheba want to deepen the connection or keep moving forward?

On the plane coming home she'd asked him again about what set him on a path to becoming a Kingpin and a member of the ruthless crime node called The Order. That wasn't a career goal anybody chose if they had a choice. And he had not chosen that life for himself. It was chosen for him....

He sat waiting for her in a small eatery called *Grand Coeur*, in the 1rst arrondissement of Gay Paree. He was dressed in European Vogue fashion. A crisp blue suit with narrow leg pants, starched white shirt, top hat and a slender bow tie. A picture of money and power. But the retired Kingpin now had a soft spot.
That spot was his one and only daughter, Sheba Ransome, his grandson Diondre and great granddaughter, Indigo.

He tapped the glass on his watch. His Sheba was late. He was about to call her when he saw her come around the corner and through the door.

To honor her father's appreciation for fashion, Sheba wore *Chanel* to their meeting. A simple black dress with a string of pearls and matching pearl earrings. Black pumps and a gold clutch complemented her ensemble. Gold bracelet on her wrist with her sparkling ten carat wedding ring.

He'd ordered them the *Grand Coeur's* famous blueberry tart and honey ice cream. The waiter was delivering steaming cups of expresso as she walked up. He rose from his seat and planted a fatherly kiss on his daughter's cheek.

They looked like a centerfold couple for a designer fashion spread. People stopped eating to try to figure out if they were part of the royal family or American celebrities. Satisfied they were just well-dressed tourists, they went back to their pre-dinner gossip.

"Daughter."

"Father."

"You look magnifico!" He said touching his fingertips to his lips and snapping his hand in the air.

"And your ensemble is flawless as always." Sheba gave him the once over.

"How was your flight? I apologize for sending you first class. My planes are being serviced."

"It was fine. Everything was wonderful."

Their small talk was irritating her. She hadn't flown all this way to make nice with him. She wanted facts.

"You must taste the dessert. *Grand Coeur* is famous around the world for this cream and blueberries."

His French accent was thick. Being home around the language brought it out even stronger.

Sheba took a few bites of the food and agreed it was the best she ever tasted.

"It is delicious. Great choice. You are well?"

"I'm finally recovering. The detective has one of his men following me when I'm in America but we lose them easily. It's like children playing with adults."
The laughed at his light humor.

"Well, I have some questions. It seems like every time we get together, I'm grilling you about something."

"We're making up for lost years. I understand. What do you need to know to have peace in your heart?"

"I need to know how come I didn't know you knew John Henry or that he used to work for you. Did we work for you at the same time?"

"There was always a window of separation. The Cartel changed leadership several times over the years. When John Henry worked for me, you were working directly for him. So I never came in contact with you. But yes, I knew he was in a relationship with my daughter. And I knew when he married you and when you gave birth to Diondre. I so wanted to be there for the birth of my grandson. I thought about telling you who I was but decided against it for Diondre's safety."

"Did John Henry know you were my father back then?"

"He had an idea but he didn't know for sure. He thought that because I was going out with your Mother, I looked out for you. After you and him split up, I tossed him some work here and there because he was desperate. Nobody in The Order would hire him because they were afraid of pissing off the top brass in the Organization. By then I was pretty high up so the Big Man turned his head when I gave John Henry a few bones to keep himself going. Those bones helped him get back in the game. He couldn't deal drugs because of the agreement he made negotiating your protection. But there was other work he did that paid damn good and was a lot safer."

"So you're saying John Henry was telling the truth about why he threw me under the bus?"

"You don't know what happened? Well, its time you know the truth. Some big Kingpin in The Order wanted the territory you developed. John Henry offered him his own top selling geography. But the Kingpin wanted *your* territory. They were jealous of your success and wanted to slow you down."
"John Henry knew that if he didn't give them what they wanted, they were coming after you. That's why he staged the big bust. He also gave it all up, everything he built, to protect you and your son."

"That's what he told me but I didn't believe him. I ended my marriage because of what they did. I mean, I lost everything because of a damn hater."

"It's over now. Fate and destiny played those cards. Who knows how things would've gone had you not went

277

through that. Sometimes, loss and endings are God's way of protecting us."

"Like me losing Mama and losing you? Was that God or was that the devil?"

"I don't know, Sheba. Maybe a little bit of both. But what I do know is, you came out on top."

"I'm going to find out who that Kingpin was that came after me and make him pay."

"Sheba, darling, that was so long ago. He's probably dead and buried in some old graveyard in New Orleans."

"You know something don't you? Tell me his name."

"This conversation is over. I didn't invite you here to talk about dead drug dealers or old vendettas. I brought you here to tell you that I've set things up so that you get everything I worked for. All those years of pain and war—I've made you and Diondre my beneficiaries. I brought copies of the paperwork for your files."

He pulled out a yellow envelope and handed it to her.

"Thank you. I…I don't know what to say."

"No thank you needed. Just go be happy. And come see your old man every now and then."

"Is there something you're trying to tell me? Are you okay? They're not after you again are they?"

"In this business, you never know. But trust that I have protection twenty-four seven for you and all those we love."

She knew what he meant by protection.

"My cleaning lady doesn't work for you does she?"

Simon fell out laughing about that.

"No, not this time."

"I'm planning a big Christmas dinner for the Indigo Family. That's what I call everybody who was on the island with us."

"I like that. Violet and I are spending a lot of time traveling and getting the businesses set up around the globe. There's a war on natural medicine and I plan to use my resources to help fight the establishment."

"She's a good woman. God really did you a favor when he gave you Violet."

"Yes He did. And you helped make that connection."

He paused for a minute as if he was contemplating something.

"His name was Two-toe Harry. The man who came after your territory. He was a Big Pin out of Louisiana who loved to turn out young girls on the Boy. Heroine that is. But I took care of him for you."

"I knew you knew something. So he's somewhere breathing dirt? Or are you just telling me that so I don't go after him?"

"You gotta start trusting me. I'm your father. I'll protect you with my life."

"That wasn't an answer but I'm gonna let the discussion drop."

"I took the day off so I could show you my city."

"Well, how about you start by taking your daughter to the museum? I've dreamed of visiting the *Louve* since high school. Mama used to talk about it all the time. She passed away before we could take the trip."

"I'd be honored to escort you. My driver is outside. Let me take care of the check and it's you and me in Gay Paree!"

When they got to the museum, Simon had arranged for an entire wing so they could browse at their leisure. They walked the halls arm and arm lavishing over the greats. Picasso, Michelangelo, Davinci—they were all there. Then they visited the Egyptian Antiquities and met the Pharoahs and busts of the African beauty, Cleopatra. Next was a collection of ritual pieces depicting indigenous African Gods and Goddesses. It was exquisite.

After visiting the Eifel Tower and attending a glorious seven course French dinner, Simon drove her to a private airport for her flight back to America.

"Can I persuade you to stay another day? I was going to take you to see Notre Dame and tour the Rose Gardens."

"Unfortunately, business demands I return to America. But how about I return with the family during the summer for an extended visit?"

"That would be incredible."

He walked over to where she was standing and opened his arms.

"Come to me."

She went to him and hugged him tightly.

"I am here for you. If you need anything, anything at all, just pick up the phone. I love you, Sheba."

"I love you too, Daddy."

They swallowed their tears and tried to part ways before they got emotional.

"That was the first time you ever called me that."

"It was the first time I ever called anybody that."

Violet got out of the back seat of a Lincoln Town Car just as Sheba was walking toward the plane.

"Shebaaaaa! I couldn't let you leave without telling you about a dream I had last night. And I have something for you. I made it. It's for your protection. It's a necklace. It'll keep you safe as you're traveling the streets of that jungle you work in."

"Thank you, Violet. This dream you had, was it good?"

"Yeah, it was good. Nothing but fish. You and fish. You know what that means right?"

"I'm going swimming or something?"

"You're probably pregnant."

Sheba fell out laughing. "I'm done with having kids."

"Well, somebody's pregnant."

"Maybe Rebecca is expecting."

"Well, there you have it. But if I were you, I wouldn't engage in playtime without a safety net."

"Thanks for the warning. You two take care of each other."

"Don't you worry, I got him."

And with that she boarded the plane. Questions answered. Heart at peace. When she sat down in her seat she felt an overwhelming urge to toss her cookies. She rushed the bathroom stall and emptied her stomach. Back in her seat, Sheba remembered Violet's dream about the fish. The flight attendant walked up with a tray. When she removed the lid, on the plate was a pregnancy test kit. Violet looked out of the window and saw her father and Violet standing on the tarmac smiling.

Violet looked up at the flight attendant and said, "I already know."

She looked out the window again and saw Violet feigning a pregnant belly.

And it was right then that Bethsheba Dorothy Ransome knew the spirits really were giving her a second chance. And this time she would get it right.

She unhooked the airplane phone and told Raymond the happy news.

"I'm going to be father. That's the best news I ever got in my life. This is the start of a new era for us."

"I'm a real bitch when I'm pregnant."

"What else is new? Did you forget that I got the medicine that'll turn your wolf into a lamb?"

Sheba started laughing. "It's the other way around. I'll have you sucking your thumb and dipping cookies into milk at the kitchen table when I get through with you."

"In your dreams, Mrs. Ogletree."

"You're the boss, Papa."

"And don't you forget it."

"You wanna know what color panties I have on?"

"Hell yeah. Let me go to the bedroom so I can take this ride the right way."